Also by Jerry Mahoney

*My Rotten Stepbrother Ruined Cinderella*
*My Rotten Stepbrother Ruined Beauty & the Beast*
*My Rotten Stepbrother Ruined Aladdin*
*My Rotten Stepbrother Ruined Snow White*

# Jerry Mahoney

Sky Pony Press
New York

First Edition

This is a work of fiction. Names, characters, places, and incidents are from the author's imagination and used fictitiously.

Sky Pony Press books may be purchased in bulk at special discounts for sales promotion, corporate gifts, fund-raising, or educational purposes. Special editions can also be created to specifications. For details, contact the Special Sales Department, Sky Pony Press, 307 West 36th Street, 11th Floor, New York, NY 10018 or info@skyhorsepublishing.com.

Sky Pony® is a registered trademark of Skyhorse Publishing, Inc.®, a Delaware corporation.

Visit our website at www.skyponypress.com.

10 9 8 7 6 5 4 3 2 1

Library of Congress Cataloging-in-Publication Data is available on file.

Cover design by Kate Gartner
Cover illustration by Chris Garbutt

Print ISBN: 978-1-5107-3261-2
Ebook ISBN: 978-1-5107-3263-6

Printed in the United States of America

For Greg,
my Lloyd

# CHAPTER 1

It only took three minor adjustments for Lloyd and me to turn a picture of our archenemy Quentin into a giant butt. First, we colored over his eyes with a Sharpie, making them into weird, ugly birthmarks. Then, we transformed his mouth into a long, thin, dangling turd. We finished it off by drawing a curved line down the middle of his nose, all the way to his chin. That was the crack. I'd like to say Lloyd and I are amazing artists, but, really, I have to give most of the credit to Quentin's face, for being so butt-like to begin with.

Once our masterpiece was finished, Lloyd held it in front of his face and did his best impression of Quentin Fairchild, the weeniest guy we know.

"Hi, I'm Quentin, and I'm a big butt!"

The high-pitched wheeze he made as he spoke sounded exactly like Quentin's horrible voice. Lloyd nailed it.

Even though we neutralized the sight of Quentin's rotten face, we still had to deal with the headline blaring at us from the magazine cover he was on: "Eleven Eleven-Year-Olds Who'll Change the World Someday." Quentin was number one on the list, of course, and I was just some loser whose mom paid $7.95 for the extra-crummy double issue.

Last year, Quentin was on a list of "Ten Ten-Year-Olds Who Hold the Future in Their Hands," and the year before that, it was "Nine Nine-Year-Olds Who Are More Successful Than You'll Ever Be, You Worthless Loser" (or something like that).

The only list I'd ever been on that was distributed publicly was a list of kids in fourth grade who had head lice. An angry mom sent it around to half the PTA when the school nurse refused to name names. That was two years ago, and everyone still remembered it. That only added to my shame at not accomplishing anything like Quentin had.

To be fair, Quentin had kind of earned all the attention. He cured feline chicken pox. You probably didn't even know cats could get chicken pox. It turns out a lot of animals can get chicken pox, which makes you wonder why they still call it chicken pox and not just "pox." It's not just a disease for poultry, like whoever named it once thought.

It happened like this: Quentin's cat got sick. He did something I still don't understand, and then his cat was cured. After that, it was like he was Stephen Hawking or cat Jesus or something. He won an award from the Veterinarians Association of America. He got to have dinner with the president at the White House. He was on the front page of the newspaper with the headline "Will This Kid Cure Cancer?" (Lloyd and I found the copy at the public library and wrote "Probably not" on it. This was before we had the artistic skills necessary to make faces into butts.)

"We should be changing the world!" Lloyd insisted as he waved Quentin's magazine cover in my face.

"But we're almost twelve!" I argued. "It's too late for us!"

It was a really good point. Everyone knows there aren't any lists of up-and-coming twelve-year-olds. Once you hit puberty, your chance to be a prodigy has passed you by. If you haven't done anything awesome by then, you might as well have been born a tree sloth or a patch of shower mold, because your importance to the planet is virtually zilch. You're never going to win a gold medal or be elected to national office, so you might as well just accept your name tag and hairnet and start shoving jalapeño horsemeat into taco shells at whatever fast-food dump will agree to hire you.

But Lloyd doesn't get upset by things like this. He gets motivated. Every time some supposedly important newsweekly declared Quentin special, Lloyd started dreaming up ways we could outdo him. He wanted him and me to be the most famous kids on Earth. So far, we weren't even in the top six billion. So this time, he decided to dream bigger. We weren't just going to be the most famous kids on Earth. We were going to be the most famous kids in the galaxy.

Maybe the universe.

We were going to be the kids who brought aliens and humans together.

With a blog.

Soon, the two of us were spending every day after school posting an online guide to our home planet, all the things that aliens should know when planning a visit here. Lloyd was sure it would convince some adventurous E.T.s to make the cross-universe trip to come hang out with us. I just thought it was fun to write. It's not like I ever believed aliens would be persuaded to come here based on something two dumb kids wrote on the freeblogz.biz domain.

And it all started by us looking at that defaced magazine cover and imagining just who our visitors might be:

http://peacefulextraterrestrialsguidetoearth.freeblogz.biz/home.html

## An Open Letter from Two Cool Earthlings to any Extraterrestrials Who Want to Visit Our Planet (but Not Kill Us)

Dear Superior Alien Race,

Hey, dudes! Thanks for checking out our blog. It should tell you everything you need to know about our awesome planet, Earth. Sure, this giant blue rock two orbits over from Jupiter has its problems: wars, hurricanes, homework. Overall, though, it's a great place to take your intergalactic vacation. We should know. We've lived here all eleven years of our lives so far. Our names are Lloyd and Josh. We're best friends, and we would be totally awesome tour guides if you want to come visit for a while.

The first thing we want to say is that if you have any plans to conquer or blow up our planet, it's small and red and has ninety-seven rings around it. It's the twelfth planet orbiting HD8673 in the Andromeda galaxy.

OK, not really, but please don't travel all the way across the universe just to destroy Earth. We kind of like it here.

Next, we apologize for writing this travel guide to our home planet via this primitive Earthling blog. We wish we could beam this message directly into your hyperevolved brain orbs, but this is the best technology we humans currently have. Believe it or not, when our parents were kids, we didn't even have tech this lame, so be grateful we're not blasting this into orbit via fax machine.

The first thing you should know about our planet is that ninety-nine percent of our so-called intelligent life here are total donkey-butt jerks. If you come to Earth for a visit, they will probably capture you, run experiments on you, and ask you all kinds of lame questions about where the universe came from and how you conquered the hurdles of intergalactic travel and what asparagus looks like on your planet. Then, you'll have to meet all these boring world leaders and give dumb speeches and take pictures with them for hours. Is it really worth having to poop in zero gravity on the long space trip just to put up with that nonsense when you get here? We think not.

By far the biggest donkey-butt jerk on our whole planet is this guy Quentin Fairchild who goes to our school. He's a nerd who hangs out with the cool kids because they think he's going to be super rich and famous someday like the nerd who started Facebook or the nerd who started the website that that guy ripped off, who later got a sweet settlement in court. The two of us are just regular nerds, who read comic books and enjoy science because sometimes stuff goes boom. Nobody expects we'll ever do anything important. So if you're going to visit Earth, come to us. We promise, when you hang out with us, no one will even notice you're here.

Quentin treats us like we're the biggest losers in the world. He always wins everything, and he loves to make fun of us because we're the only ones who still bother to compete against him. Josh ran against him for student body president, and Quentin wasn't happy just to beat him. He told half his voters to vote for a rock just so Josh would come in third. Now Josh is known as the guy who lost to a rock. Granted, if the rock can't fulfill its duties for any reason, Josh will move up a slot, but that's not looking likely. It's a big rock, and it's not going anywhere.

That's why we came up with the idea for this online guide to our home planet. Once you see how awesome Earth is, we know you'll want to come stay with us for a while. That will make us way cooler than Quentin. Plus, we'll show you all the awesome stuff our planet has to offer, like pizzas that cook in ninety seconds and bike hockey (which is a game we made up that's like hockey, but on bikes) and Generation: Scream, which is this totally sick suspension coaster where your legs dangle out and you go so fast that there's a sonic boom and so high that you have to breathe oxygen through a face mask. It's at a theme park called Thrillington Palace, and it doesn't open until next summer, but trust us, it's going to be humankind's greatest accomplishment yet, and we're the species that came up with the idea of putting yogurt in tubes, so that's saying something.

We've thought a lot about what you must look like, and here's our best guess: You're probably about three feet tall, with butts in the back of your heads. You're scaly in front and furry in back, with spikes down the sides of your arms. You have nine fingers on one hand and four fingers on the other, plus a third hand with no fingers at all and a belly button in the middle. Or maybe it's an ear. We're not sure about that one. You have two eyes, just like us, but you can swap them out with your friends if you want to see what they're seeing.

It goes without saying that you're crazy smart, because you probably have about twenty brains each, including a mini brain in each of your toes. You probably speak like five languages, including your language, English like us, and something really hard like Dutch or the language ants use to tell each other where the rotting rat corpses are. You've come up with a way to play tic-tac-toe so that it's not always a tie, and you can read a whole book in one second just by holding it up to one of your toe brains, even if it's a really boring book about life in the Old West or something.

As for us, your Earth hosts, we each have two eyes, two arms and, when you put both of us together, over two hundred Star Wars toys. What could be cooler than that, right?

Hope to see you soon. Hyperwarp safely.

Sincerely,
Lloyd Ruggles
Joshua James McBain III

Posted by Lloyd and Josh, September 8 at 7:12 pm
Likes: 4
Comments: 0

Brilliant, right?[1] If you were an alien, you'd totally want to meet those guys, wouldn't you?

---

[1] Ugh, footnotes! Is this really going to be that kind of book? Well, don't worry. These footnotes are actually kind of cool. Whenever you see one, it means Lloyd and I wrote a blog post to explain that topic to aliens, and the footnote will tell you what page at the end of the book to flip to if you want to read it. Yeah, I know, the only thing worse than footnotes in a book is an appendix. I won't blame you if you throw this book in the garbage right now.

There was definitely one place where our obsession with aliens came in handy, and that was with our science teacher, Mr. Mudd. He was supposed to be teaching us about all kinds of science, but mostly, he talked about outer space. Mr. Mudd had a very strong connection to everything beyond Earth and very little connection to anything on it. I thought I'd impress him by doing my oral report on comets, but Lloyd tried to warn me against it. "Mr. Mudd will be bored," he insisted.

I was convinced Lloyd was wrong. I researched the crap out of comets and found out they were actually totally awesome. I ended up having to do the presentation on my birthday, which I figured was a good sign. Who gets a bad grade on their birthday?

"Comets have been streaming through our solar system since the formation of the sun," I told the classroom, standing in front of a papier-mâché replica of the comet Hale-Bopp. I thought that was a pretty cool fact, but when I looked over at Mr. Mudd, he was gazing out the window with disinterest. I had to get his attention fast or I was going to flunk.

"Halley's comet sightings happen only once every seventy-six years," I explained, "but believe it or not, Halley's is considered a short-period comet. Comet Hyakutake was last visible in 1996, but astronomers believe it may not return for seventy thousand years!" I saw lots of kids nodding in amazement, but when I glanced over at Mr. Mudd, he was nodding off at his desk. My report was actually putting him to sleep. I needed some comic relief, quick. "Seventy thousand years," I continued, "or roughly as old as the meatloaf they're serving in the cafeteria today." I got a big laugh on that line. That settled it. Comedy was the way to go.

"Comets are made up of rock, dust, and high concentrations of frozen gases like methane and ammonia," I told the class, "which means, in all likelihood, comets smell like farts." I had built in a pause in my presentation, figuring I'd get a huge laugh at that point, after which Mr. Mudd would have to tell everyone to settle down. As it turned out, I only needed half the pause I expected. The fart line got a big laugh, but all Mr. Mudd did was roll his eyes.

It was only when I wrapped up my presentation five torturous minutes later that Mr. Mudd finally looked up, yawning as he marked down my grade. "B-minus," he droned.

Of course, that got the biggest laugh of all.

As I sat back down, Lloyd shook his head, consolingly. "I told you that wouldn't impress him."

Mr. Mudd was not a typical teacher, that's for sure. He had hair like Albert Einstein. It defied gravity, sticking up in every possible direction. Like a fingerprint or a snowflake, it never took the same shape twice. His clothes never matched. Today, he was wearing a pink-and-purple polka-dot shirt with yellow-and-red plaid pants. It was almost like he went to his closet and grabbed the top half of one clown costume and the bottom half of another. He wore glasses with one lens as thick as a first-generation iPod, and the other side had no lens at all because that eye had perfect vision. He always had at least one visible booger, and we could all see it because no matter what he was looking at, his head seemed to tilt slightly backward at all times. It goes without saying that he smelled worse than a comet. Maybe that's why he didn't like my joke.

While other science classes dissected worms and studied how sodas could eat the tarnish off a penny, we focused almost totally on astronomy. And most of that was devoted to alien conspiracy theories like the spaceship that supposedly crashed at Area 51. For weeks, Mr. Mudd discussed the inconsistencies in official CIA statements about the incident and showed us blurry videos from the 1970s of weird objects in the sky. "That doesn't look like a weather balloon to me!" he would rant.

Some people joked that Mr. Mudd himself was from another planet.

If he was, Lloyd seemed to be happy visiting him there for a while.

"What is this bizarre, unearthly object?" Lloyd asked, as he began his presentation to the class. He projected a photo onto the Smart Board. It showed a weirdly shaped something or other silhouetted against the clouds, high above Earth. It was made up of two round, egg-like halves, with a ridge running down the middle. People started giggling, not because this whole report was ridiculous, which it was, but because the object Lloyd was speaking so seriously about looked like a gigantic butt.

"No one knows for sure," Lloyd continued, "but it's been spotted hovering around our planet for decades now, perhaps even for millennia." He flipped through a few other photos of the object in different positions in the sky, ending on a drawing of cavemen pointing at the doohickey in prehistoric times. Meanwhile, he underscored his presentation with creepy techno music to give it a mysterious feel.

Mr. Mudd was riveted. He was leaning so far forward in his chair that it looked like he was trying to climb over his desk. "Yes?" he said, eager to hear more. "Yes? Yes?"

"Scientists have yet to give it a name, but I call it the Gluteus Extraterrestrius. The Space Butt."

This got a big laugh—from everyone except Mr. Mudd. "NASA once commented on this satellite, you know," he said.

"Oh, I know," Lloyd replied. "They called it a fragment from an ancient comet. But why would a piece of a comet look like two bulging cheeks and a crack, am I right?"

Mr. Mudd nodded enthusiastically. I quietly rolled my eyes. Lloyd was so good at this.

"No one knows its origin . . . or its purpose." Lloyd dimmed the lights. The music grew louder and louder while only a flashlight beam shined on Lloyd's panicked face. He was really getting dramatic now. "Was it put in the skies above us by humans? Impossible.

It weighs ten tons, far too much for our meager technology to have put it there way back when it was first sighted. The only plausible explanation is that it came from someone more advanced than us."

Lloyd flipped to a picture of an alien out of an old black-and-white sci-fi movie.

"Yesssss!" Mr. Mudd hissed.

"Are they spying on us? Certainly. Manipulating us? Possibly. Planning to take over the Earth?" He switched off the projector and shrugged. "Who am I to say? All I know is, whoever they are, they're listening to us right now, to this very report. So let me ask them . . ."

He raised his head up to the sky as if speaking directly to the aliens who were supposedly eavesdropping on his science report. "WHAT ARE YOU PLANNING, GIANT SPACE BUTT?" he shouted.

Then, the lights went out, the music cut off, and there was total silence.

The next sound we heard was Mr. Mudd jumping up and applauding. "Brilliant!" he said. "Amazing!"

Lloyd had not said a single fact that could be found in a textbook, except that NASA declared this was all a complete crock. Yet it was exactly what our teacher wanted to hear. "A-plus!" Mr. Mudd enthused.

Lloyd returned to his seat, smirking at me. "That's how you do it," he said.

"You didn't say anything but nonsense," I whispered. "You just said what he wanted to hear."

"Exactly," Lloyd replied.

Mr. Mudd turned the Smart Board back on. "I've always been fascinated by this particular unidentified orbiting object. And I'm impressed with all the photographs you found!" He flipped through Lloyd's pictures of the weird sky thing. "You even found one I've never seen before." He focused on a photo of the Space Butt passing in front of the moon.

"Oh, that?" Lloyd said. He motioned toward me and smiled. "Well, I have to be honest. Josh actually came across that one while he was researching his report. You can really see the division between the two cheeks on that one. Right, Josh?"

Lloyd winked at me to get me to play along. "Um, yeah. The left cheek seems especially suspicious," I agreed.

Mr. Mudd nodded at me, impressed. "Nice work, Josh. Just for that, I'm bumping you up to an A-minus." He made a note in his grade book, and Lloyd high-fived me.

"Happy birthday, Josh," he said.

Man, Lloyd was the best.

❂

If the A-plus wasn't enough evidence, I could tell how well Lloyd did on his report by how annoyed everyone else in the class was at him. After the bell rang, while we were leaving the room, pretty much everyone was muttering under his or her breath. Things like, "I worked for a month on my presentation!" And, "I should've done my report on Ewoks." And, "Next year, I'm taking chemistry." I couldn't help thinking that moments like this explained why Lloyd and I had never quite broken through to the top tier of popularity.

"We're the talk of the class!" Lloyd beamed. Sometimes, it amazed me how the two of us were able to see the same situation completely differently.

As we entered the cafeteria, Kaitlyn Wien-Tomita came scooting up to us with her camera rolling. Kaitlyn was pretty cool—in my mind, at least. (Of course, that probably meant she wasn't very cool as far as most other kids were concerned.)

Kaitlyn had one of those fancy action cameras you could clip on to a snowboard or a white-water raft to capture your extreme sporting adventures. That's not what she used hers for, though. Kaitlyn had a YouTube channel. She'd had it since second grade. Back then, she was obsessed with these toys called Purse Puppies. Each one was a stuffed dog that you carried around inside a faux designer pocketbook. Like they had a Pomeranian inside a gold purse with a label that said POOCHI instead of GUCCI. She used to do reviews of all the new ones that came out, and sometimes she would play with them and make up little stories where they solved crimes or went to tea parties.

Not a lot of people watched her channel, but the company who made Purse Puppies heard about it, and they sent her a free French bulldog in a Hair-mès bag, a week before they sold it in stores. After that, tons of kids at school started their own channels where they played with their toys, but nobody else got any freebies, so eventually they all stopped. Except Kaitlyn. She grew out of Purse Puppies, of course. Now she was interested in Lloyd's report for some reason.

"Lloyd, that was quite a presentation you gave today," Kaitlyn said as she focused her lens on us. "Care to comment?"

"Happy to, Kaitlyn," Lloyd replied. "I'm fascinated

by the mysteries of the universe, and today, I was humbled to do my tiny part to illuminate one of the most mysterious of all, the Space Butt."

Kaitlyn nodded. "So you believe in aliens?"

"Absolutely," Lloyd answered. "The universe is far more vast than our tiny human brains can comprehend. Seems like that'd be an awful lot of wasted space if it was just us here." Most kids wouldn't be so open about believing in aliens, but I guess Lloyd wasn't worried what people would think—or maybe he just figured no one would ever see this, so it didn't matter. "I try to remember that, to everyone else in the universe, it's we here on Earth who are the aliens." I had to back away a bit so that Kaitlyn wouldn't catch me rolling my eyes on camera.

"So if they're watching us right now," Kaitlyn continued, "what message would you want to give them?"

"I'd tell them to come hang out with me and Josh. We're the coolest guys on Earth!"

Kaitlyn shut her camera off. "Thanks, guys."

"What's this for?" I asked her. "You doing videos about aliens now?" It seemed strange, because I couldn't imagine what kind of free products she might get for that.

"More like local news," she said. "I'm training to be a reporter, like Stacy Diaz-Finch of Channel 8."

"Ah," I said. "Good luck."

"Yeah, there aren't many big stories around here." She shrugged. "But I'll keep trying. It's good practice, if nothing else. And if aliens do come visit you and Josh, I hope you'll give me the exclusive."

She said it with a wink, and I think she was expecting Lloyd to make a joke in response. Instead, he replied, with complete earnestness, "Oh no, Kaitlyn. I could never betray an alien's trust."

Kaitlyn backed away slowly, eyeing Lloyd like he was a lunatic. "I'd better get to my fourth period," she said.

I thought Lloyd was a little nutty, too, but as it turned out, I wouldn't be thinking that for much longer.

# CHAPTER 2

Every day, my parents put a note in my lunch bag. The notes are always really corny, like they'll draw a cartoon of a man in a suit of armor, and they'll write, "See you to-KNIGHT!" The notes mean so much to them. It's always the first question they ask me at dinner. "What'd you think of the note today?" I usually try to answer with my mouth full of food, so I don't have to lie.

"Ihh wuff hurrblll," I'll answer, and they'll smile proudly.

"Thanks!"

On the morning of my birthday[2], I was bracing myself for a particularly atrocious note, because my parents always go totally overboard celebrating my birth. I

---

2   See page 247 for our blog post about Earth's five bajillion holidays.

wouldn't have been surprised if I opened my lunch and confetti popped out while a tiny speaker played my dad singing "For He's a Jolly Good Fellow." Much to my relief, it was just a regular note, which said, "Choppy birthday to our favorite boy!"

It took me a minute to get it, and then I got really excited.

"Lloyd!" I shouted. "Look!"

Lloyd glanced at my note and shook his head. "Your parents are weird."

"Don't you get it? Choppy birthday. That means they're taking us to Chop Socky!"

"Aw, sweet!" Lloyd said.

Chop Socky was a Japanese restaurant on Route 48, but the good kind of Japanese restaurant, the kind where they cook the food right in front of you, as opposed to not at all. There's a giant grill at every table, and instead of them bringing the food out from the kitchen when it's ready to eat, they let you watch them make it. I think once everyone heard about sushi, Japanese chefs had to create restaurants like this. When you know that a chef likes to serve things raw, you want them to prove to you that they're actually cooking your meal:

Of course, cooking food is boring, so they amp it up by juggling knives and making volcanoes out of onions. Pretty much everyone who goes to Chop Socky is having a birthday, because you can get the same food at Tokyo Town at the mall food court for about 1/100th the price, but without the possibility that your cook might accidentally slice his hand off while making it.

Of course, I always bring Lloyd along on my birthday dinners because he never really gets to celebrate his own birthday. He's the youngest of nine kids, so by the time he came along, his parents were tired of throwing parties. It was always one kid's birthday or another, and besides, there was never enough cake to go around. One year, they held a raffle to determine which kids would get cake on Lloyd's birthday. Lloyd lost. He had to blow out a candle wedged between two saltine crackers and a slice of American cheese. After that, he told his parents not to bother anymore.

✪

The first thing I noticed when the waitress sat us down was how familiar our chef seemed. His name tag said Hiroshi, but I was pretty sure I had never met a Hiroshi in my life. When my mom saw him, she squealed with joy.

"Teddy?" she said.

"Hi, Mrs. McBain," Hiroshi replied.

My dad stared at the guy, confused. "Who's this?"

"Oh, Don, you remember Teddy Woo, don't you? He used to mow our lawn."

"They call me Hiroshi here," Teddy said. My mom ran around the hibachi to give Hiroshi/Teddy a hug. She asked how his parents were, then he told her he was majoring in history at the University of Delaware, and then he asked my mom if she wanted white or brown rice with her combo platter.

Teddy/Hiroshi was a really good chef. He made a smiley face on the grill in oil, and then he set it on fire. He made two shrimps look like they were dancing together to the Taylor Swift song playing on the speaker system. He shouted out Japanese phrases with the enthusiasm of someone who'd just won a hundred thousand dollars on a game show.

One thing that stinks about Chop Socky is that even though it's your birthday, they still make you eat vegetables. Next to the chicken and the noodles, Hiroshi cooked up a big, steaming pile of broccoli. Yuck. Broccoli doesn't even deserve to be called a vegetable, if you ask me, because I'm convinced it was never intended to be edible. Sure, it comes out of the ground, but so do rocks and sand. Broccoli is a much closer relative to them than it is to carrots or corn, which I can at least swallow without gagging. In my mind, the only good reason to eat broccoli is in the hope that someday we'll eat it all, and it'll be wiped off the face of the Earth.

The chefs at Chop Socky try to make eating broccoli "fun" by turning it into a game. After they cook it, they fling it with a spatula over the grill, and you try to catch it in your mouth. It's pretty much the worst game ever, because the only prize for winning is getting to eat broccoli. Thankfully, Lloyd had come up with a great plan to beat the broccoli game.

We watched my mom try about five times to catch the broccoli in her mouth, while my dad shouted, "Come on, Debbie!" at her. Finally, she caught one, and we all cheered.

My dad got his on the first try, and he stood up to take a bow. "Come on, Hiroshi! Give me another one!" he said. Then, he caught that one, too. "One more! I'm on a roll!" he said. He ate four pieces of broccoli before he finally missed one. Hiroshi bowed to him in respect for his broccoli-catching skill.

Then, it was my turn. Lloyd winked at me, reminding me to do exactly as he'd told me. Hiroshi flung a floret at me, and I jerked my head around like a maniac so it looked like I was trying to catch it, but then I missed on purpose. "Aw," my dad said. "Give him another chance!"

Hiroshi flung a second piece of broccoli at me, and I did the same thing. Another miss. "Keep trying, Hiroshi!" my dad said. "He'll get one!"

I missed another piece, and another. My dad started laughing. "C'mon, Josh," he said. "It's not that hard." A small forest of broccoli was building up at the base of my stool.

Soon, half the restaurant was watching and cheering me on.

They must've heard my dad say my name, because they started chanting, "Jah-osh! Jah-osh!" (It took me a minute to realize that "Jah-osh" was supposed to be "Josh." You really need at least two syllables in your name for it to be chantable.)

Hiroshi would fling, I would miss, and everyone in a five-table radius of us would go, "Aww!" Then, the cycle would repeat. "Jah-osh!" Fling, miss, "Aww!" "Jah-osh!" Fling, miss, "Aww!" You'd think my dad would've caught on, but all he kept saying was, "Wow, Josh. You are really not good at catching broccoli in your mouth!"

From across the room, I saw Kaitlyn Wien-Tomita, who was dining with her mom, dad, and grandma. Kaitlyn had her camera trained right on me. I could just imagine this going viral. "Broccoli klutz epic fail." Thankfully, Hiroshi was onto me. By the time the twentieth piece of broccoli had fallen on the floor, he said, "I'm sorry. The manager won't let me throw any more broccoli to this boy without charging you extra."

"Nice try, son," my dad said. "Well, maybe Lloyd'll get one!"

"Oh no. I can't," Lloyd said.

"What do you mean?"

"I'm cabbage intolerant." Man, my best friend was a genius.

"Cabbage intolerant?" my dad repeated.

"Yeah, broccoli is part of the cabbage family. So is cauliflower, radish, turnip. I can't eat any of them."

"What would happen if you did?" my dad asked.

"I would barf my guts out," Lloyd said.

What made the broccoli game even more painful was that I was desperate to get to the main course: my present. Since I was about two years old, I'd been begging my parents for an iPhone[3]. But they read some article in a parenting magazine that said the best age to get your kids a phone was twelve, so they kept telling me I had to wait. Lloyd knew he'd never get an iPhone, at least not until Apple came out with something newer and cooler and one of his older brothers gave him a decade-old iPhone that was destined for the garbage. That meant all our hopes of joining Bueller Middle School's tech-savvy elite rested on my shoulders.

Finally, as Hiroshi wiped the grease off the grill, my dad reached down for the iPhone-shaped package at the foot of his stool.

"Thank you!" I shouted, ripping open the wrapping paper before he even handed it to me.

"I'm guessing you know what this is," my dad said.

I'm not sure, but I think when I first saw it, I made a sound only dogs could hear. It was the most high-pitched squeal I'd ever made in my life. There, in my hands, was my own iPhone. Shiny, perfect, mine.

"Whoa!" Hiroshi said, impressed. "That's the newest one. You guys must've waited in line hours for that!"

---

3  We talk all about iPhones (and other, less-cool inventions) in our blog on page 248.

My mom smiled and put her arm around me. "Josh is worth it. We love him so much!"

"Turn it on," my dad said. "We loaded it with games for you."

I swiped my finger across the screen and saw app after magnificent app. All the best games were there. *Catch the Donkey, Extreme Bubble Wars, Zombie Pizza Parlor,* and about fifty different versions of *Angry Birds.*

"Do you like it?" my mom asked.

"I love you!" I said, giving her and my dad a huge hug. I could've hugged them all night, but I didn't want to spend that long apart from my new iPhone.

"Hiroshi, will you take a picture of us?" my mom asked.

"No, Mom, don't you know anything about iPhones? We'll just take a selfie!" I opened the camera app and reversed the lens, as if I'd been doing it my whole life. I couldn't believe it. My first selfie. I stood between my parents, and Lloyd leaned over to photobomb us. I had to stretch my arm way out to fit us all in the frame. "Hold on. Move in a little tighter," I said. I tilted the camera back and forth trying to get just the right angle. "OK, hold still." I had never actually taken a selfie before, and it was only when my arm was stretched out as far as it could go that I realized I didn't have a free finger to snap the picture with.

I took my index finger off the edge of the phone and tapped the shutter button, but as I did, the phone came loose and fell out of my hand.

"NOOOOOO!" I screamed. It seemed to happen in slow motion, as my brand-new, beautiful, perfect iPhone plummeted at full speed toward the ground.

# CHAPTER 3

My mom gasped. Lloyd dove for the phone, but it was too late. It kept falling toward what was sure to be a brutal, untimely death.

Only it didn't die. It just stopped falling somehow. There was no thud or crash, only a soft little *squish* sound. When I looked down to find it, there it was, sitting safely on top of all that broccoli that Hiroshi had flung at me. It was a small mountain of disgustingness, with my gorgeous iOS device at its peak, unharmed.

"I don't believe it!" I said. "The broccoli broke its fall!"

"It's a Chop Socky miracle!" Lloyd said, high-fiving me.

I picked up the phone, and there wasn't a crack on it. It turned on. The camera app had even saved the picture I took, although it was a little blurry because it was falling as the shutter snapped and my mouth was wide open because I'd just started to scream. But the phone was now coated with a weird slimy gunk. "Oh, yuck!" I said. "Chop socky sauce!"

"Here, let me wipe that with my napkin," my mom said.

"Oh no, Mrs. McBain," Lloyd said, grabbing the iPhone away. "We'd better take this to the bathroom[4] and clean it very carefully. C'mon, Josh."

I followed Lloyd to the bathroom, knowing he had more in mind than just cleaning the iPhone off. The whole way there, he was flipping through screens and checking things out.

"Lloyd, what are you doing?"

"Nobody knows your new phone number yet. We have to pull some pranks!"

"Who are you pranking?"

"Duh. Quentin. He puts his number on his website so news crews can contact him." Lloyd took a close-up of his mouth sticking out his tongue and texted it to Quentin. "Ooh, that'll drive him crazy!"

---

4   See page 249 for our blog on human bathrooms, the only place on Earth where it's OK to poop.

By then, we reached the bathrooms, but I stopped short as I stared at the two doors.

"Go in!" Lloyd said.

"But, Lloyd, which one is the men's room?"

I hate when restaurants try to be clever on their bathroom doors, like at the seafood restaurant where they say "Gulls" and "Buoys" or at the Down Under Grill, where they say "Sheilas" and "Blokes." Sorry, but when my butt is about to explode from eating your food, I don't have time to stop and appreciate your puns.

At Chop Socky, the bathrooms had Japanese writing on them, which might as well be pictures of Japanese people laughing at me because I was never going to figure out which one was the men's room. Underneath the writing were anime characters, one of which was supposed to be a boy and one of which was supposed to be a girl. But they both had long hair and gigantic eyes with stars in their pupils, so I couldn't tell them apart.

"Just pick one," Lloyd said. "You have a fifty-fifty chance of getting it right."

"Right," I said, "and a fifty-fifty chance of being the weirdo who walked into the girls' room and got yelled at by somebody's mom."

"It's that one," Lloyd announced, confidently. He pointed to the door on the left.

"Why do you think that?"

"Look at the other one. It has boobs."

I looked closer at the door on the right, but I didn't see any boobs.

"No it doesn't!"

"Trust me. Boobs look different in anime."

I sighed. By this point, no one had come out of either door and we hadn't heard any flushing, so that meant the bathrooms were probably empty. All I had to do was crack the door open and see if the place was a total mess with pee on the floor and paper towels overflowing the garbage can. That's what men's rooms looked like, in my experience. Women's rooms were much nicer, which I knew because my mom always made me go to the bathroom with her in public until just last year, when I said I'd rather pee my pants than go into a women's bathroom with her one more time.

I went up to the door on the left and gently pushed it open. To my horror, there was someone inside—a kid using the sink, but he or she was facing the other way and I couldn't tell from behind if it was a boy or a girl. Thankfully, they didn't see me standing there trying to figure out which sex they were. That would've been pretty embarrassing for both of us. They were short, though, shorter than me, and wearing a hoodie that covered the back of their head.

When I looked closer at the hands, there was something very strange about them. They were covered with fur on one side and scales on the other. One hand had nine fingers and the other had four. Then there was a third hand with no fingers at all but a belly button in the middle. Or maybe an ear. I wasn't sure.

As I stood there, staring, the whatever-it-was turned around and faced me, and that's when I realized this was no kid at all. It was an alien, with a huge, scaly head and enormous eyes and four round things on its neck that were probably ears.

I closed the door and backed away.

Lloyd was laughing, but he wasn't laughing at me. He was staring at the iPhone screen. "Quentin just wrote back, 'Who is this?' Ha! We got him!"

I grabbed the iPhone away from him. "Lloyd, there's something in there."

Lloyd gasped. "Was it the girls' room?"

"I don't know," I answered.

"Well, who was in there, a girl or a boy?"

"I don't know," I said again. "Lloyd, it wasn't human."

"You're kidding! Is there a rat or a possum in there? People are going to freak out!"

"No, it wasn't a rat or a possum. I think . . . I think it was an alien."

"Oh, ha ha, Josh. We both know you're not much of a prankster, so you should leave the jokes to me."

"It's not a joke," I assured him.

Lloyd sighed. "Fine, I'll take a look. I'll even pretend I believe you if that makes you feel good." He stepped forward and pushed the door.

The alien was waiting for him, waving happily. "Bike hockey?" it said.

That settled it. It was definitely an alien, and he'd read our Earth travel blog!

Lloyd was speechless, and as his jaw dropped, the iPhone slipped out of his hands. This time, there was no broccoli on the floor to break its fall. It landed with a nasty cracking sound. The screen shattered instantly. A huge spiderweb–shaped crack spread across it.

If that wasn't the worst moment of my life, then what came next was, as three squishy alien hands reached out and picked up the phone. The creature pulled it in for a close look, then backed away and closed the bathroom door behind him.

Just like that, my brand new iPhone was gone.

# CHAPTER 4

Back when we wrote our blog, Lloyd and I spent a lot of time wondering what aliens might be like. Curious, probably. Unarmed, hopefully. One thing we'd never imagined, though, was that they would be lousy stinking iPhone thieves.

Now here I was at my favorite restaurant outside either the men's or women's room—I still wasn't sure—seething over some three-armed blob from outer space who stole my birthday present. We'd just solved one of the greatest mysteries of human existence. Yes, there was life in outer space.

And they were total jerk faces.

What could we do, though? The alien was an advanced life-form who had mastered interplanetary space travel, and Lloyd and I were just two sixth graders faking our way through science class. We were way outmatched. I turned to Lloyd and could see from the look on his face that he was thinking the same thing I was. I opened my mouth to say, "Let's get out of here," and at that moment, Lloyd opened his mouth, and said . . .

"Let's go get him!"

"Lloyd, he could vaporize us!"

"Good!" Lloyd said.

"Good? How is that good?"

"Because we Earthlings stick together. There's one of him and seven point three billion of us. If this sets off an intergalactic space war, so be it. Humans versus the lowlife E.T. scum. Haven't you seen any movies about aliens? We always kick their butts in the end. Someday, kids will learn about this moment in school. It'll come right after the question on history tests about how Archduke What's-His-Name's assassination started World War I. Universe War I began when what unbelievably brave kid got vaporized at the Chop Socky on Route 48? And you know whose name squijillions of future children will write in the blank?"

"Yours?" I said hopefully.

"No," Lloyd replied, dramatically. "They'll write Joshua James McBain III!"

Lloyd could be really good at convincing you of things. As he stared at me encouragingly, I actually got stirred up inside. I felt pride for my planet. I was an Earthling, darn it, and I had to stand up for that big beautiful blue marble I called home. "Besides," Lloyd added, "do you really want to go on living without an iPhone?"

"OK," I said. I slapped my hands against the bathroom door and got ready to push. "Let's go."

But instead of striding confidently up behind me, Lloyd took a step back.

"One of us has to survive to tell the story of your heroism," he said meekly.

I grabbed him by the arm. "Come on!" Yanking Lloyd behind me, I pushed open the door and entered. I took a second to look around and saw that the walls were pink, and there were no urinals or mysterious puddles on the floor.

"Dude," Lloyd said, confirming my worst fears. "This is totally the ladies' room."

The alien stared at us, and all my courage disappeared in about a half second. He was small and funny-looking, but I had no idea what he was capable of. I shielded my head with my arms and whimpered, "Please don't vaporize us!"

The alien took a step toward us, and then we heard a voice coming from behind him. "Hey, dudes!" it said. "High five!" The alien held up all three of his weird hands. I looked at Lloyd and he shrugged, then went ahead and slapped each one with his palm. So there it was. A historic moment. Humans had finally made contact with extraterrestrial life, and it was me and Lloyd in the women's bathroom at Chop Socky. I would always be a very special member of the human race. The Abraham Lincoln of alien contact, the Isaac Newton of interplanetary communication.

Suddenly, Mr. Mudd didn't seem so crazy, and I realized Lloyd was right for always believing this moment would happen. I decided I should never doubt Lloyd again.

"I can't believe we're actually meeting Lloyd and Josh!" the voice said. I wanted to be flattered that I'd achieved this level of fame in outer space, but I was starting to get really frustrated that I couldn't figure out where the voice was coming from.

"Are you talking to us?" I asked.

"Yeah, dude," the alien laughed. "You're just looking at the wrong place. Our mouths are where your butts are."

Lloyd burst out laughing. "No way!"

The alien turned around, revealing a thick pelt of blue-green fur that stretched from his neck down to his feet. In the middle of it all, where his legs came together and his butt should've been, was a perfectly ordinary, almost human-looking mouth.

"Way!" the butt-mouth said, enthusiastically, revealing three rows of green, goopy teeth.

Lloyd and I were pretty impressed. "But where do you poop from?" Lloyd asked.

"Duh, my butt!" the alien said, and with one of his hands, he pointed up toward the back of his head. Sure enough, there was a long, deep crack running down the middle of it.

"That's your butt?" I said in awe.

"Don't believe me?" his mouth said. "How about now?" Then I saw the most amazing thing I'd ever witnessed. As Lloyd and I watched with our mouths hanging open and our eyes bulging in shock, the cheeks of the alien's head-butt quivered like pudding and out came a blaring, unmistakable trumpeting sound: FRRRRRRRT!

We had met an alien, and we watched him fart. This day couldn't get any cooler.

"You were right!" I said to Lloyd. "They do have butts in the back of their heads!"

"Yeah, we read that on your blog. That's how we knew you guys were cool," the alien said. "On most planets, they think buttheads like us are weird."

Lloyd shook his head dramatically. "I can honestly say, your head is the coolest thing I've ever seen."

"Thanks. Now stop staring at my butt!" the alien scolded, turning around.

Lloyd turned to me, patting me on the back. "So they're exactly like we imagined!" he said. "We're geniuses!"

"Not exactly," the alien said. He held up his third hand and pointed to the thing in the middle of it. "See this?"

"Yeah, is that a belly button or an ear? We weren't sure."

"It's a dimple. It only shows up when we smile. See?"

He frowned with his butt-mouth and the dimple went away.

"Cool!" Lloyd said.

The dimple reappeared, and the alien started laughing. "A belly button on our hands! We thought that was hilarious!"

Meeting an alien was exciting, but I still wanted my iPhone back. "Um, do you have that cool, shiny device you just grabbed away from me?" I asked.

"Sure do!" the alien said. "It's in my butt."

"What?"

"Here you go!" the alien cheerfully announced, and he reached one of his hands through his butt crack, felt around for a second, and then delicately pulled out my phone.

"Eww!" I said.

"Awesome!" Lloyd gasped.

The alien held the phone out, and I backed nervously away. I'd spent years begging my parents for this, and now, just a few minutes after I finally got it, it had already been destroyed and then put inside an alien's rear end. Did I still even want it?

"Don't freak out," the butt-mouth said. "Our butts do lots of stuff. They're not just poop chutes like yours." I took a look at the phone. Every trace of the cracks on the screen had been wiped away somehow. It looked just as fresh as if it had come right out of the box.

"You got rid of its cracks," Lloyd gasped, "by sticking it in your crack."

I grabbed the phone, no longer caring where he'd yanked it out of. I touched the home button and the screen lit up, as good as new.

"Your butt is awesome," Lloyd said. "You really are a superior race."

I couldn't help myself. I lunged forward and wrapped my arms around this strange space creature as tightly as I could. Yes, I hugged an alien. I guess it was a bold step forward for humanity. It was definitely a closer encounter than I'd ever expected to have. Two species from across the galaxies had come together in a sign of peace and love.

It didn't feel quite as good as getting an iPhone did, but it was definitely the second-best moment of my birthday.

And then I heard someone going to the bathroom.

"FRRT!"

I looked at the alien in surprise. "Someone's in here!" I said. "You'd better hide!"

"It's OK," the alien said. "He's with me."

He pushed open a stall door, and I almost fell over when I saw what was inside. There, with the back of his head resting on the toilet seat, was another alien. It took me a second to realize what he was doing with his head on a toilet seat, but of course, it was exactly what you would expect someone would do on a toilet seat if they had a butt on their head. I looked away quickly, and heard a mighty trumpet blast. "FRRT!" Then came a plop, and the alien sighed in relief.

"You said your butts weren't poop chutes!" I said.

"I said they weren't *just* poop chutes," the alien replied. "They can repair small electronics, but they also blast dookies."

He closed the stall door, and just then, we heard someone coming down the hallway. Before we could react, she had pushed the bathroom door open. Lloyd and I both dove for it, but it was too late. We saw her, an old Japanese lady, looking directly at us, two boys in the ladies' bathroom.

She started to scream.

"Um, just a minute!" Lloyd said. He pushed her backward into the hallway, while I closed and locked the door behind her.

"That's Kaitlyn Wien-Tomita's grandma!" I whispered. "She saw us!"

"*Ma, Shinji rarenai wa!*" the woman shouted. She

pounded on the door harder, yelling at us in another language. "*Wa, ano koe wa otokono koe da wa!*"

"Oh no! She's speaking Japanese!"

Lloyd shook his head. "Yeah, and she totally knows we're dudes!"

As Lloyd and I wondered what to do, we felt three hands reach out and push us aside. The alien stepped forward, bent over, and spoke through his butt mouth in a perfect Japanese accent. "*Gomennasai. Watashi no yujin wa hidoi geri de komatte imasu.*"

"*Ara sore wa yoku nai desune. Daijobuyo, machimasho,*" the woman said.

Lloyd and I were both majorly impressed. "Your butt speaks Japanese?"

"Yes," he said. "I am fluent in Earth."

"Earth? You mean like every language people have?"

"Not just people. Dogs, porcupines, caterpillars. I know every language spoken on your planet. I can even understand when grown-ups talk about politics."

"Wow! You guys are geniuses!" I said.

"I have been speaking to you in adolescent boy dialect. It's a combination of rap lyrics, language we picked up from your blog, and dialogue from sitcoms starring obnoxious teenagers. We on fleek, yo?"

"No one really says that anymore," I said.

"We may need to do some updating, home slice." Then, he extended two of his hands, holding one out to me and one to Lloyd. "Wanna know my name?" he asked. "IAmAWeenieBurger."

"You are?" Lloyd wondered.

"You seem pretty cool," I said.

He stared at us confused, then burst out laughing. "Oh, right! I forgot that IAmAWeenieBurger means something different in your language. On our planet, IAmAWeenieBurger is a very common name, like Mike or Joe. Some of our finest minds are named IAmAWeenieBurger."

From inside the stall, a toilet flushed, and out waddled the other alien. "This is my buddy," IAmAWeenieBurger said, "Doodoofartmama."

Lloyd laughed. "Doodoofartmama? Is that a common name on your planet, too?"

"Nah," IAmAWeenieBurger said. "His parents are a little weird."

Doodoofartmama held up his hands for a high five, but I backed away. "Um, on our planet we wash our hands after going to the bathroom."

Doodoofartmama turned toward IAmAWeenie-

Burger, confused, and he farted. IAmAWeenieBurger farted back at him.

"Sorry, yo," IAmAWeenieBurger said. "The doodoo man doesn't speak Earth as well as I do, so I translated to our language."

"You speak in farts?" Lloyd said. "Gross!"

"Well, we think it's gross that when humans talk, everyone can see all the nasty stuff in your mouth," IAmAWeenieBurger said. "Tongues? Blecch!"

"Touché." I nodded.

"But how do you know what anybody's saying?" Lloyd asked. "Aren't all farts pretty much the same?"

IAmAWeenieBurger laughed so loud he farted again. "You humans really are so simple. Farts can be distinguished based on a complex assessment of pitch, tone, and duration. I should know. I studied fartguistics in buttiversary. Oh, plus they all smell different."

"You speak in smells?"

"Yes! If I want to say, 'I am delighted to make your acquaintance, kind sir!' the smell that comes out is like a combination of earwax and prune juice. FRRT!"

"Ugh, nasty!"

"Or if I want to say, 'What a lovely planet you have

here, Earthlings!' I blast out a butt bomb not unlike an elderly middle school teacher's perfume. FRRT!"

Out came the worst stink known to human-kind. It smelled exactly like my math teacher, Mrs. Schermerhorn. I started gagging, just like I did every time Mrs. Schermerhorn walked right by my desk. "How do you say 'I think I'm going to throw up'?"

"That one actually smells like warm cinnamon buns. FRRT!" In an instant, Lloyd and I were surrounded by the sweet odor of icing-drizzled baked goodness. I would never have guessed it was produced by an alien's rear end.

"Mmmm!" Lloyd said as he savored the scent.

"You really are an advanced species!" I added.

Doodoofartmama began farting excitedly. "FRRT! FRRT!" These were quick blasts that stank of seafood on burnt toast.

"Shhh!" IAmAWeenieBurger scolded him. "You took the class on human behavior, too! First, we need to make small talk." He turned toward us, trying to be casual. "So, did you see last night's episode of that TV show we all enjoy?"

"What's he so excited about?" Lloyd asked, plugging his nose so he wouldn't have to smell what Doodoofartmama was saying.

IAmAWeenieBurger sighed. "He wants to talk about video games[5]."

"FRRT!" Doodoofartmama replied, hopping up and down. "FRRT! FRRT!" The seafood on burnt toast smell returned, even stronger.

"OK, OK, we get it!" I said, fanning the air with my hand to clear out the stench.

IAmAWeenieBurger stepped forward. "The last time we came to Earth was in your year 1984. We got really hooked on a game called *Pac-Man*. We heard he got married, and now there's a Ms. Pac-Man!"

"Oh, we've come a long way as a life-form since then," Lloyd said. "Josh has the new PlayStation! Did you guys get that on your planet yet?"

IAmAWeenieBurger shook his head, sadly. "We don't have any video games on our planet."

"Dude," Lloyd said. "What an awful place to live."

"But you guys are so much smarter than us," I said. "You know how to fix things with your butts. How come you haven't invented video games?"

IAmAWeenieBurger sighed. "We've spent all our time working on space travel, curing diseases, and

---

5  On page 251 we blog about all kinds of games, the video kind and the lamer kind, too.

creating a sustainable environment. You humans, on the other hand, have focused on making weapons and games and drugs that cure baldness."

"Well, come over to Josh's house!" Lloyd said. "You can play any game you want! He has everything!"

"FRRT!" Doodoofartmama farted, cheering up.

"Lloyd!" I whispered. "What about your house?"

"No, it should be your house. You have better video games."

"But my parents would kill me! No one will even notice them at your house. There are so many people there, they'll blend right in!"

"But, Josh—"

"But, Lloyd—"

Without warning, two massive jets of dark blue fluid spouted from the alien's eyes and shot across the bathroom, splashing me in the face. "Boo hoo hoo!" he whimpered. "I feel unwanted!"

"Aw, Josh. How could you?" Lloyd said. "You made IAmAWeenieBurger cry."

"Look, I'm sorry," I said. "But my parents really don't like overnight guests."

"FRRT?" Doodoofartmama farted, wondering what was going on.

"FRRT," IAmAWeenieBurger explained, tearily. "FRRT FRRT FRRT." Out came a soft, weak sputter that smelled like dried mud.

"Waaaah!" Doodoofartmama bawled, and his eyes spewed out tears, too, washing over me like a downpour. I was drenched.

"OK, fine!" I said, standing under the automatic hand dryer. "You can stay at my house. But my parents can't know."

"Hooray!" IAmAWeenieBurger cheered. Then, he turned to Doodoofartmama to explain. "FRRT FRRT!" he said.

Just as I stepped out from under the hand dryer, I was blasted by another tear tsunami. "Why is he still crying?" I asked, wringing the alien tears from my T-shirt.

IAmAWeenieBurger sniffled happily. "Those are tears of joy," he said.

# CHAPTER 5

Lloyd promised he'd come up with a plan for how to get two aliens from the ladies' room of Chop Socky to my house at 439 Elm Street without causing an international incident. He slipped out of the bathroom to investigate the area, and I was left babysitting the two overgrown space weirdos by myself while I awaited his instructions. Thankfully, Doodoofartmama was completely entranced by the hand dryer. He was using it to blow out his fur, emitting a strange humming noise as he stood underneath it. I think he may have been in love.

"You have so many cool toys on your planet," IAmAWeenieBurger said as he watched his friend geek out under the nozzle.

I realized how easy it would be to impress him with all the stuff humans have invented. "That's nothing," I said. "Watch this!" I stuck my hands under the faucet, and the water automatically turned on.

"Ah yes!" IAmAWeenieBurger said. "I was admiring your water dispensing device when you entered the bathroom."

"Yeah, the technology is pretty advanced," I said. "I'm not sure you'd understand it."

He leaned down and inspected the sink. "Actually, it's pretty obvious. When the infrared proximity sensor is triggered, it uses electromagnetics to open the solenoid valve, initiating the flow of water."

"Um, yeah," I replied. "Something like that."

"Neat." He patted me on the head.

"I still can't believe someone actually read our blog," I said.

"Well, we always clicked the 'like' button on your posts so you would know."

"So that was you? Cool!"

"FRRT!" Doodoofartmama added, his flatulence reeking of envelope glue. His fur was all blown out from the hand dryer. He looked like a troll doll, albeit one with a butt on its head.

"But wait," I said. "All of our posts got four likes. If you guys were the first two, I wonder who the third and fourth likes were."

IAmAWeenieBurger shrugged. "I'm pretty sure they were not buttheads. Most of us have terrible net-iquette. So tell me. How can we make you cooler than the donkey-butt jerk named Quentin?"

"You'd really do that?" I couldn't help smiling. Lloyd and I were going to be heroes. "First, let's just worry about getting back to my house."

"Do you really think Lloyd will come up with a good plan?"

"Don't worry," I said. "If there's a way, Lloyd will find it." I couldn't imagine what he might come up with, but I knew it would be genius.

A minute later, Lloyd was back, dragging a double stroller through the ladies' room doorway.

"Lloyd, where did you get that?"

Lloyd shrugged. "This place keeps a whole bunch of 'em out front for their customers. It's pretty cool of them."

"Those belong to people!"

He shrugged again. "Then we'll go fast."

"We can't put the aliens in there!" I said.

"Of course not," Lloyd replied. "But we can put your 'baby brothers' in there. C'mon, guys!" He boosted Doodoofartmama into one side of the stroller. His tiny three-foot-tall frame was a perfect fit. He could totally have passed for my little brother.

To someone who was completely blind, at least.

"Um, Lloyd, you don't think anyone's going to notice that my baby brothers are green and scaly and, um, cheek-headed?"

"Not on such a chilly night," Lloyd said. "They'll be wrapped in their baby blankets." He took a couple of blankets out of the bottom of the stroller. They had pictures of trains and rubber duckies on them, along with lots of spit-up stains. "Here, guys. Get cozy." Lloyd handed the blankets to the aliens, and they started wrapping themselves up.

"But how will I get them into the car? I don't have the keys."

"Please!" Lloyd said. "Like I've never pickpocketed before?" He held up my dad's keys proudly and tossed them to me.

"You are right," IAmAWeenieBurger said. "He is a genius!"

"FRRT!" Doodoofartmama agreed.

"It's a good plan, Lloyd," I said. "But while I'm pushing the stroller, what are you going to do?"

"I'm going to create a distraction so you can sneak out."

"How?" I said.

"I'll need your phone." I handed over my iPhone, then Lloyd ducked back out the bathroom door to get to work.

I strapped Doodoofartmama and IAmAWeenie-Burger into the stroller, making sure they were fully covered up with the blankets. Then, I pulled the canopies down as low as I could over their heads. I had to admit, they were a little big for babies, but no one would ever have known that they were anything but human underneath. Satisfied, I took a deep breath and opened the bathroom door.

I could hear Lloyd making a commotion, and by the time I got to the lobby I could see him standing at the front of the dining room. He had put a chef's hat on his head and was commanding everyone's attention.

"Thank you for coming to Chop Socky tonight!" he said, as if he actually worked there. "We have a very special birthday we want to celebrate. Stand up, Mrs. Tomita!"

He pointed across the room at Kaitlyn Wien-Tomita's

grandma. When she realized everyone was looking at her, she scowled angrily and said something in Japanese. Kaitlyn seemed to think it was awesome that someone was embarrassing her grandma, so she started encouraging her to stand up.

"Oh, don't be shy now!" Lloyd said. He strode up beside her and helped Mrs. Tomita to her feet. "To celebrate this special day, let's all dance to Mrs. Tomita's favorite song from her youth."

The next thing I knew, Lloyd was blasting an old school jam sung in Japanese from my iPhone.

The confused grandma gazed around her as everyone boogied in her honor. My parents, the bartender, even Hiroshi was joining in. Kaitlyn whipped out her camera and started recording. No one was looking in my direction, so I pushed the stroller out the front door. Finally, Kaitlyn's grandma gave in and joined the party.

As the door closed behind me, I realized that what Lloyd had succeeded in getting everyone in the restaurant to dance to was not this woman's favorite childhood song. It was probably just the first hit on YouTube for "1950s Japan dance music" or something like that. But he fooled everyone else and charmed Mrs. Tomita into playing along. He had done his part. Now I just had to get these aliens into my parents' trunk.

That's when I saw the other strollers lined up outside the restaurant. There was a whole stroller parking area, beside the waiting bench and the pillar of sand that people stub their cigarettes out on. It was then that I first considered the fact that whoever owned this stroller might actually come looking for it.

A police officer walked toward me. Was he coming to get me? Oh, God. I was a criminal now! A stroller thief! My heart started racing and I stopped short, ready to stick my arms out for the officer to slap handcuffs on. But as he got closer to me, the cop actually smiled. "Aren't you a good big brother?" he said, and he passed by me with a wink.

I breathed a sigh of relief and shoved the stroller over the curb onto the asphalt. I didn't want to take any chances now. I had to hurry. I could see my dad's Mini Cooper, just two rows over. I was almost there. I was almost free. Then, I heard a voice.

"Oh, let me see the little sweetie pies!"

It was an old lady[6] with a walker. I'm never good at guessing people's age, but I'm pretty sure she was at

---

6   You probably don't want to read a blog about old ladies, but trust us, it's surprisingly awesome, just like old ladies themselves. See page 253 and we'll tell you why.

least a hundred and fifty. She had glasses so thick they made her eyes look like flying saucers floating above her head. Her hair was curly and white, and the look on her face said she thought I was just the cutest thing ever.

"I really need to go," I said. I tried to push past her, but she blocked my way with her walker.

"How old are they?" she asked.

"Um . . . sixty-eight months?" I said. I knew parents always talked about their kids' age in months, and it wasn't until I spat the number out that I realized I had just told this lady there were two five-year-olds in this baby carriage.

"Twins?" she gushed. Thankfully, she was no math whiz.

"Uh-huh," I nodded.

"Identical or fraternal?" she asked.

I knew those were two kinds of twins, but I wasn't sure which answer would make this woman go away faster.

"Um, both?" I said.

"What?" she replied. Apparently, that was not an acceptable answer. I was totally busted. I had to think fast. I decided to do what Lloyd always did when he was in danger of getting caught: change the subject.

"How many grandkids do you have?"

It's a can't-fail plan with old ladies. Get them talking about their grandkids, and you're home free. You can zone out for the next hour, and they'll still be talking. Soon, she was telling me all about Brandon's yellow belt in tae kwon do and the three goals Miley scored in soccer last week, as if I actually knew these people and cared about their accomplishments.

I slowly began to back up. Maybe I could slip away without her even noticing I was gone.

Sure enough, she kept talking, moving on to other subjects. Disrespectful teenagers, arthritis, rap music. She was actually able to rant about two things at once, like social security and swearing in movies. "I paid into that system for fifty years, so they'd better not cut my funds, and I don't understand why they can't use nice language anymore!" she said. It was impressive, really. She was old lady-ing on a very advanced level.

"Where are you going?" she said finally, when I had made it about two car lengths away from her.

"My brothers are tired," I said. "I really need to get them home."

"Aw," she said. "Little angels. Just lemme get a li'l peek at their precious li'l faces." She clattered closer to me with her walker. I knew she'd scream if she took off the blankets and found herself face-to-butt with an alien's rear end crack.

"That's not a good idea!" I warned, but she ignored me and started leaning down toward Doodoofartmama. There were at least a thousand ways I could've stopped her. I could've tackled her or turned and run. I could've called for the police or told her to mind her own darn business.

I just hate to make old people sad. She was so nice. Where was Lloyd when I needed him?

I closed my eyes and braced myself as she reached her wrinkled old fingers down and tugged at the blanket covering Doodoofartmama's face. Then, just as it was about to fall off and reveal his scaly green complexion, he farted.

"FRRRRRRRRRT!" he blared.

"Oh my!" the old lady giggled. "Sounds like he's a little busy! Better leave him to his business."

She backed away from him, and I breathed a sigh of relief, but just for a second.

"Let's see his brother instead," she said. She reached toward IAmAWeenieBurger, and I cringed.

That's when I heard a voice coming from the back of the stroller. "The senior discount ends at eight p.m.," it said.

"Oh, phooey!" the old lady shouted. "Gotta go!" She wheeled around, lifted her walker, and scooted as fast as her legs would go toward the restaurant.

I sighed in relief. "Nice work, IAmAWeenieBurger," I said.

"I told you I speak every language on your planet," he replied. "Even old lady."

Thankfully, there was no one else between me and my dad's Mini Cooper. I popped the trunk and squeezed my extraterrestrial stowaways in, hiding them underneath the reusable shopping bags.

"Is this the part of your vehicles you ride in?" IAmAWeenieBurger asked me as he fumbled clumsily to fold his arms inside the trunk.

"No, but this is the part *you* ride in," I explained. "Sorry. Will you be OK in here?"

"No problem," IAmAWeenieBurger assured me. "We will simply go number four."

"Number four?"

"Oh, right. I forgot you humans only have two ways to go to the bathroom."

"How many do you have?"

"One hundred and forty-two. Some are just for special occasions."

"Whoa!" I'd never felt so ashamed of my species and how much evolving we still had to do.

I wanted to ask what number four was, but then I saw a woman wagging her finger at me from the restaurant's front door. "There it is!" she wailed. She held two babies in her arms. "What are you doing with my stroller?" she demanded.

Kaitlyn was just leaving the restaurant when she saw this going down, so she took out her camera to catch the scene, as I quickly slammed the trunk shut. "I— I—" I stammered.

The woman was furious. "Thief!" she yelled. "THIEF!"

I couldn't move. All I could do was stand there looking guilty and thinking about what a horrible person I was. I had stolen this woman's stroller, after all. So much for my near-perfect track record as a good citizen.

I was about to confess everything, when my mom came out of the restaurant looking for me. "Josh?" she said, as she spotted me, red-faced, about twenty feet away.

"Is this your son?" the angry mom asked. "I caught him trying to steal my stroller!"

I cringed, wondering how my mom might react. Would she burst out crying because her son was a criminal, or would she scream at me first? Instead, she did neither.

"How dare you!" she shouted at the angry mom. "To accuse my son of something like that, on his birthday, no less! Now, I don't know what the story is here, but I can assure you my son did not steal your stroller. My son doesn't do bad things. Before you make accusations like that, you should give him a chance to explain."

"Fine," the woman huffed. "Explain!" She turned to me and waited, her arms crossed defiantly. Beside her, my mom nodded her head at me, smiling encouragingly. And next to her, Kaitlyn zoomed in for a close-up.

"Well. . ." I said, stalling. I couldn't confess now, not with my mom's trust on the line. Then, right on cue, a hero swooped in to save the day.

"Josh! Did you get him?" Lloyd came running up behind my mom, acting as if he'd been looking all over for me.

The angry mom and I both turned toward him, baffled. "Get who?" we said.

"The thief," Lloyd explained. "The stroller thief. We saw this big creepy-looking weirdo trying to run away with your Ultra Oopsy Baby, ma'am. Everyone's after this stroller." He turned and looked directly into Kaitlyn's camera, with a wink. "It's the hottest stroller on the market."

"Oh, I know," the woman said, proudly. "It was out of stock everywhere. I paid a fortune for it online! Only the best for my twins!"

"And you can thank my friend for saving it," Lloyd told her.

The woman smiled at me. "Well, thank you!" she said, a bit flustered.

Once again, I was amazed at Lloyd's skill. "No need for reward money," Lloyd assured her. "Just the look on those cute little angels' faces is all we need. C'mon, Josh."

Lloyd started to lead me back into the restaurant. Kaitlyn stopped recording and grabbed her grandma by the arm. "You guys are fun!" she said, laughing, as she walked her grandma to their car.

My mom wasn't quite ready to leave, though. "One more thing," she hissed at the stroller mom. "You owe my son an apology!"

The lady bowed her head, ashamed. "I'm very sorry, young man. You're a hero!"

"I told you," my mom said. "My Josh is a good boy." She winked at me, proudly, then walked back inside the restaurant.

"I don't know if I'd use the word 'hero,'" I started to say, acting as humble as possible. I felt Lloyd tugging on my arm. The woman was putting her babies into the stroller now, and Lloyd was eager for us to sneak away while she had her back to us.

He yanked me toward the front door, and as I followed him inside, I heard the woman say, "Where did this blue fur come from?"

"Just keep walking," Lloyd advised me, and soon we were back at the table eating fried ice cream with my parents, while Lloyd snuck the keys back into my dad's pocket.

The first part of the plan was a success. Now all we had to do was get home and sneak the aliens inside.

# CHAPTER 6

Being in my parents' car was like being in prison, only worse, because at least in prison, you don't have to listen to the '80s channel on the radio. I didn't know any of the songs, but Mom and Dad swore each one was the greatest song ever. I have no idea if anyone from the '80s was actually a good singer, because my parents always drown them out with their own off-key howling. This one was about some woman who was working as a waitress in a cocktail bar, and Lloyd and I wanted to jump out the window.

"I'm sorry," I typed on my iPhone screen, then I passed it to him so he could see.

"The aliens aren't going to be so peaceful after listening to this," he wrote back.

My dad sang some refrain about whether or not Mom was going to change her mind, or they'd both be sorry, and I typed something that had been on my mind: *My mom was SO mad at that stroller lady!*

Lloyd read what I wrote and typed a reply: *They trust you.* He smiled at me, then added another sentence: *Use it to your advantage.*

I wasn't sure exactly what he meant by that, but he was right about my parents. They thought I could do no wrong.

Lloyd took the phone back. He pulled up an emoji of a skunk holding its nose and saying, "P.U.!" Then, he wrote, *What's that smell?* I took a whiff, and sure enough, there was a pretty strong stench in the Mini Cooper. I'd describe it as halfway between moldy cheese and a new shower curtain when it first comes out of the package.

*The aliens are going number four*, I wrote back, then I added an emoji of some guy shrugging. I passed him back the phone and, while he read my message, I marveled at how cool technology was. Before tonight, Lloyd and I would never have been able to talk about aliens two feet away from my parents like this.

*What's number four?* Lloyd wrote.

I thought it over for a second. *Something smelly*, I typed back.

My dad turned around to see what Lloyd and I were doing. "You guys playing a good game back there on the new phone?"

"Yeah," Lloyd said, pretending to tap at the iPhone screen. "It's called *Stinky Aliens*."

"Ha!" my dad laughed. "Those games have some funny names!"

We pulled up in Lloyd's driveway behind his family's bus. Lloyd's family was so big, they had to buy a small bus so they could cart everyone around. It wouldn't be so bad if they hadn't painted the side with caricatures of each of the kids and the words Team Ruggles in giant letters, like they're a family singing group on tour or something. If they go to the mall, when they come out, there are always people taking pictures of their van. There's even a Tumblr page where people put up pictures of themselves pointing at the van and laughing.

"Want me to walk you in?" my mom asked.

"Nah, that's OK," Lloyd said, and I could see how relieved my mom was. My parents and Lloyd's parents don't really like each other, and they try to avoid each other whenever possible. It's weird, because grown-ups aren't supposed to be cliquey like kids. Neither Lloyd nor I can tell whose parents are the cool ones. Each of us is pretty sure it's the other's.

"Good luck tonight," Lloyd said to me as he left the car.

"Good luck?" my dad asked.

"With the Stinky Aliens," Lloyd nodded. Man, was he good.

As soon as we got home, my parents started complaining about their jobs. "I'm going to get slammed at the office tomorrow! I just know it!" my dad groaned.

My mom dragged her feet across the carpet, like she'd instantly lost all her energy just thinking about it. "I can't believe the night is over!"

It wouldn't have been so annoying if they didn't do this every single night. It usually began about one minute after they got home. For roughly sixty seconds, they would tell me how happy they were to see me and how glad they were that work was over. Then, their joy would disappear in an instant and they'd start griping about having to go back to their offices the next day. It's like they hadn't realized until that moment that time would continue to move forward.

My dad patted me on the back. "I hope you had a good time tonight," he said.

"Yeah," my mom agreed. "Birthdays are a great reminder of what life is all about." Then, in case I missed the point, she added, "Life is not about work."

I was powerless against their self-pity. All I could do was ride it out, wondering the whole time how much number four-ing IAmAWeenieBurger and Doodoofartmama could do in the trunk of the tiniest car in the world.

"Tomorrow's my staff meeting," my mom pouted.

My dad put his arm around her. "Are you giving a presentation?"

She whimpered like a sad puppy. "Yes!"

Roughly five bajillion groans and gripes later, they were finally dressed in their pajamas and kissing me good night. As soon as their light went out, I sprinted downstairs and out the front door.

As I approached the Mini Cooper, I saw the trunk overflowing with an odd-colored ooze. It was a mix of brown, orange, and red I had only seen one other place on Earth—in the Crayola 64 pack. When I colored as a kid, I always wondered what the "burnt sienna" crayon was supposed to be for, and now, for the first time, I had encountered it in nature. Burnt sienna ooze was everywhere, dripping over the license plate and puddling on the driveway.

I was starting to understand what number four was, and it was even grosser than number one or number two.

The sludge had already burst through the lock, and all I could see inside the trunk was a deep pool of the stuff, swirling around the spare tire, chunky like gravy. I gazed around to make sure no one on my block was outside, then I bent down and tried to spot any sign of alien life amid the gunk.

"IAmAWeenieBurger?" I called into the goop, and I certainly felt like one. "Doodoofartmama?" Two sets of eyes bubbled up to the surface of the sludge and gazed back at me. "What are you guys doing?"

"I told you we'd be going number four," said a voice, gurgling up from the goo. "Jump in! It's fun!"

"No thanks," I said. "And can you come out now? It's really nasty."

"Of course," IAmAWeenieBurger said. His eyes rose up on a hill of slime, and around them formed IAmAWeenieBurger's head. It was an incredible sight. He turned from a gel to a solid, as his body molded itself back into the shape it had earlier. He was remade in burnt sienna gunk before my eyes, then as I watched, he turned back to his original greenish-blue color, just the way he was when I first met him. The fluffy blue fur sprouted right back out of his skin.

I checked around to make sure none of the neighbors could see the buttheaded, half-jellied extraterrestrial in my driveway. "We need to get you inside, fast."

"FRRT!" IAmAWeenieBurger called into the trunk. "FRRT! FRRT!" Doodoofartmama began to climb out of the trunk ooze, retaking his original shape just as his friend had done.

"Let's go!" I urged, but as I pushed them toward the front door, I saw that the trunk was still full of slime. It gripped the sides and curled around the taillights. A trickle of it oozed toward the gutter in the street. It was everywhere, and it reeked. "Can you do something about that crud?" I asked.

"Oh, don't worry," IAmAWeenieBurger replied. "Number four dissolves on its own." I started to relax, until he added, "Over the course of, like, ten Earth years."

"What? It has to be gone by tomorrow morning when my parents wake up."

"Oh, no way." He shook his head. "It's a real pain to clean."

"FRRT?" Doodoofartmama asked.

"What did he say?"

IAmAWeenieBurger smiled. "He's wondering if we can play video games."

All I could think at that moment was: *Getting revenge on Quentin had better be worth it.*

❂

I set IAmAWeenieBurger up on the PlayStation, and I gave Doodoofartmama my iPhone. I showed him a game called *Ultimate PukeCoaster*, which I heard some cool kids at school saying was fun. You get to build your own roller coasters and add all the loops, corkscrews, and sudden stops you want. The goal is to earn barf points by making them so maniacal that people throw up while riding them. The only thing that's kind of annoying is that they make you wait to build each new ride, and it can be hours before you get your theme park going. Still, I had no idea how long it would take me to get the alien gunk out of my parents' Mini Cooper, so I figured he had some time.

I tried not to think about what I was cleaning up. It wasn't exactly poo or pee, but it would definitely have been at home alongside them in a sewer or a human intestine. I decided to pretend it was Nutella. So although it was horribly disgusting, I could at least bear to touch it.

First, I tried Windex, because that was my dad's solution to most messes in the house. It always took the stickiness out of spilled orange juice, and it even wiped out the smell that time I barfed up my bean burrito in bed. Unfortunately, though, its cleaning superpowers turned out to be limited to disgusting Earth messes. When I used it on the trunk gunk, it only made it thicker and smellier.

I returned to the driveway with a can of Ajax, an industrial-scented powder you shake out of a can. I sprinkled a little on the mess, but the mess clearly didn't like it, because it spat it back at me.

Next, I rubbed the gunk with the stuff my mom uses to clean the bathroom tiles, and it started crackling and spewing out an orange-colored smoke. I had to duck for cover behind the tool cabinet for five minutes until it finally settled back down.

It was no use. I tried every spray, powder, and gel,

but nothing seemed to cut through the thick, sticky yuckiness. I collapsed onto the driveway with my head in my hands, wondering how I'd ever face my parents in the morning.

My options were severely limited. I couldn't tell them the truth, that I had allowed aliens to undergo some revolting excretory function in the trunk of their car. And I couldn't think of any other explanations for the goo. I wished Lloyd had an iPhone so I could text him. He'd be able to think of something. The only thought that came to my mind was to pack a suitcase and ask IAmAWeenieBurger and Doodoofartmama to take me back to their planet with them.

Right now, that was Plan A.

I lay down on the asphalt. It was after midnight now, and I was defeated and exhausted. I decided I'd go to sleep right there and hope that everything would sort itself out magically by morning. Just as I closed my eyes, I felt something run across my chest.

"Hey!" I shouted. I bolted upright as a squirrel scurried up to the puddle of goo on the driveway and began licking it. "Get away from that!" I shooed, and the squirrel scampered off.

When he was gone, I noticed he had taken a big

chunk of number four with him. He sat underneath a tree and nibbled it like it was an apple or some other delicious treat. Man, animals are disgusting. A few seconds later, he had swallowed the whole thing and was coming back for seconds.

"Get away!" I shouted. Then I stopped myself. The squirrel was doing exactly what needed to be done. He was destroying the evidence. Sure, he was possibly contaminating himself with some toxic otherworldly byproduct, but that was his problem, not mine. I stepped back and waved him in. "Come on!" I said. "Pig out!"

Seconds later, there were two dozen squirrels hopping around like maniacs inside the trunk of my parents' car. They were crawling over each other to get to every last drop of alien discharge the way Lloyd's brothers and sisters did when their mom put out a bowl of hot dog mac and cheese casserole. It was a slimy squirrel smorgasbord, an all-you-can-eat barf-out buffet for yard rodents, and they loved it. One by one, they skittered away, back to whatever gutter or sappy tree hole they had crawled out of, leaving behind a trunk that had been completely picked clean. Where all the cleaning products had failed, squirrel spit had succeeded. Finally, I could go to bed.

I rounded up my supplies and marched triumphantly to the front door. As soon as I entered, I was barraged by the sound of laser guns, rockets, and IAmAWeenieBurger laughing his butt off while playing a video game. Good thing my parents were deep sleepers.

"Wow, you made it to Saturn?" I said.

"Oh yes!" IAmAWeenieBurger cheered. He zapped the waddling, acid-spitting space aliens one after another, cackling with glee as their guts splattered across the TV screen. "Take that, space jerks!"

I was a little annoyed to see how far he had progressed. I'd been playing *Galacto Blast 7* for weeks and was still stuck on Mars.

IAmAWeenieBurger took aim at a giant space slug and blasted him to smithereens, then the screen went dark and the end credits rolled. "What's this?" he asked.

"Whoa, you finished the game." I was impressed for about half a second, and then I was annoyed. While I was purging his putrid intestinal muck from my parents' car, my extraterrestrial guest was overwriting my save file and kicking my butt. Now, I'd have to start the game all over again. "Was it at least cool?" I asked.

"It was AWESOME SAUCE!" IAmAWeenieBurger said.

I turned to Doodoofartmama, wondering what he had ruined while I was gone. "Are you still playing *Ultimate PukeCoaster?*" He was obsessively tapping his many fingers on the screen to collect puke points from around his theme park. He was so entranced, he barely even acknowledged me.

"Frrt . . ." Doodoofartmama droned.

"Oh, he's, like, totally addicted to that app," IAmAWeenieBurger said.

From looking at the screen, I could see how much Doodoofartmama had accomplished in the game. He had dozens of coasters built, each with an almost uncountable number of twists, hills, and loops. From what I'd heard, it could take days just to get your first coaster up and running. "How did you build so many coasters so fast?" I asked him.

He showed me a button he could tap, marked "Regurgitation Station." It took him to a store where he could buy puke points . . . for real money. Like, 40 points cost $1.99, 110 points cost $4.99, all the way up to 3,000 puke points, which cost $99.99. That one was labeled "Best Deal."

"You didn't buy those, did you?" I asked.

Doodoofartmama had a guilty look on his face.

"You can't do that," I said. "That's real money. That's a lot of real money. How much did you spend?"

Doodoofartmama shrugged and went back to tapping the screen to collect puke from around his theme park. I grabbed the phone away from him. "I think that's enough for today," I sighed. "Let's go to bed."

I moaned and walked over to take the TV remote from IAmAWeenieBurger. Just as I bent down to get it, I felt my shoe sink into something deep and sticky. "Yuck!" I looked down to find my shoe sunk into a disgusting puddle of unknown green goop. "What is that?" I said.

"Beats me," IAmAWeenieBurger said, shrugging. "Never seen it before."

"FRRT!" Doodoofartmama added.

"Ah," IAmAWeenieBurger said, translating. "It came out of Doodoofartmama's toes."

"His toes?" I said. "How could that possibly have come out of his—"

"Uhh-SHOOZ!"

Doodoofartmama made a weird sound, and a whole mess of the same green goop came shooting out of his toes. It drenched me up to my ankles.

"Ugh!" I groaned.

"Gnarly!" IAmAWeenieBurger said. "What was that?"

I stepped out of the puddle, wondering if I'd ever be able to get my sneakers clean or if I'd have to burn them. "It sounded like a sneeze."

The aliens both gasped, then applauded happily. "We have always wanted to sneeze!"

"You've never sneezed?"

"No. We have no germs on our planet. There's nothing to make us sick[7]."

"Wow," I said. "That must be cool. But wait, it couldn't be a sneeze. Sneezes come from your nose, and that came from his feet."

"Butthat'swhereournosesare!" IAmAWeenieBurger explained. "Look!"

"What?" I bent down, and sure enough, the aliens' big toes each had two nostrils in them. "That's amazing! And weird."

"It makes sense to have your smelling organ as far away from your butt as you can get it, doesn't it?"

I got down on the floor and looked right into Doodoofartmama's left toe-nose. They were just like human nostrils, with tiny hairs inside and even a

---

7   Wanna read our sickest blog ever? See page 255.

couple of boogers clinging to the walls. As I was checking them out, the nostrils began to wiggle and take in air. "What's it doing now?" I asked.

"Uhh-SHOOZ!"

A giant snot rocket shot out of Doodoofartmama's toes, right at my face. It was all over me, dripping down onto my shirt. It smelled, tasted, and felt absolutely disgusting.

"FRRT?" Doodoofartmama said.

"Is he apologizing?" I asked, as I tried to pick his mucus out of my hair.

"No, he's asking if we can play some more games while you clean it up."

# CHAPTER 7

Don't ever have a sleepover[8] with an alien.

It might sound cool to observe an extraterrestrial's sleep habits, but I'll spare you the trouble because I've done it myself, and it was pretty much the worst six and a half hours of my life. For one thing, the buttheads glowed in the dark. Brightly. Lying next to IAmAWeenieBurger and Doodoofartmama was like having a spotlight shone directly on me all night long. It would've been easier to fall asleep while listening to Katy Perry belting out "Firework" in Madison Square Garden, only that might actually have been quieter. That's because aliens also hum in their sleep. Just a soft, constant drone all night long. The humming

---

8   See page 257 for our blog on sleep, the easiest thing humans do all day.

wasn't that bad, honestly, except that at random intervals, it suddenly turned into an unbearable, ear-piercing screech, like the high note in "Firework." I'm not saying I didn't fall asleep. Over the course of the night, I probably fell asleep five hundred times, but only for three to twelve seconds each time.

While the buttheads glowed, their skin became see-through, and I could look at all the organs inside their bodies, which was even creepier than it sounds. They had four lungs, six hearts—which, unlike ours, were actually heart-shaped—and what appeared to be a merry-go-round circling their stomach. It actually had little horse-shaped objects that moved up and down as they went around. I'm sure it served some vital bodily function for their species, but I kept expecting one of their kidneys to hop on for a ride.

Before I knew it, it was 6:59, and I had less than one minute to wake up. We have a rule in our house that I need to be out of bed at 7:00 a.m. sharp. It has nothing to do with how long it takes me to get ready for school. It's just that my mom read on a website that it's important to spend at least forty minutes of quality time with your children every morning, and she and my dad leave at 7:40 to go to work.

I'm not allowed to set an alarm, either, because my dad saw a talk show hosted by a doctor who said the first thing you hear in the morning sets the tone for your entire day. Since alarm clocks make awful sounds, if that's what wakes you up, you'll have an awful day. Like if your alarm clock buzzes, I guess the idea is that you could spend all day swatting at bees. Of course, I find that unlikely, but who am I to argue with a TV doctor/talk show host?

So, no alarms. I just have to wake up at 7:00 a.m., or else. The "or else" is a special kind of torture I wouldn't wish on any twelve-year-old on Earth. I'm so afraid of it that I automatically wake up between 6:54 and 6:57 every day. Somehow, my mind just senses the imminent doom and sends a message for me to get out of bed, pronto.

Except today. My restless night threw everything off, and now it was 6:59. There was no time to flee. I had to move fast. "You guys!" I said, nudging the buttheads awake. "Hide!"

"Uhhrrrrrgggrr!" IAmAWeenieBurger muttered, half awake. "Wanna sleep more . . ."

"Hurry!" I tossed him off the bed. "They're coming!" I could hear my parents' footsteps on the stairs.

87

I pushed the aliens with all my might under my bed. This was what I always did with stuff I didn't want my parents to see. I just shoved it under my bed and let my comforter hang down low to block it. Unfortunately, today was the day my brilliant plan finally imploded before my eyes. There was too much junk under my bed for the buttheads to fit there.

"Ow! Ow!" IAmAWeenieBurger whimpered as I pushed him against the bed frame.

"Hey, Don, do you know what time it is?" my mom said from the hallway, as she reached the top of the staircase. Oh no. It was starting.

"I sure do, Debbie!" my dad responded happily.

I grabbed IAmAWeenieBurger by the shoulders, pleading. "I need you to go number four!"

"If you say so . . ." he replied, and he and Dood oofartmama dissolved instantly into burnt sienna–hued goo. They slithered in among the other stuff under my bed, and I pulled the comforter down so my parents couldn't see them. I then leapt back into bed, just as my parents danced in from the hallway with giant Mickey Mouse smiles on their faces.

"It's wakey wakey time!" they sang together in hideous harmony.

Then, they started dancing and shaking their jazz hands. It was a song they made up called "The Wakey Wakey Song," and it was every nightmare I've ever had rolled into one.

"Goodness sakey!" my mom sang.

"Flip some pancakeys!" harmonized my dad.

"Say bye-bye bed and hello eggs and bakey!"

This was my punishment for not getting out of bed faster. An overly rehearsed a cappella wake-up song, which my mom and dad had routinely performed for me every day of my life from birth until I begged them to stop, around age five. Since then, they've only done it when I overslept, which is why I never oversleep.

Usually.

"Wakey wakey! Wakey wakey!" They leapt up on my bed and started tap-dancing on my mattress.

"It's OK," I assured them. "I'm awake." I had to stop them before my dad got to his rap solo.

"Oh, all right, sleepyhead!" my mom said, climbing down. My parents high-fived, then tap-danced back to my doorway.

I've been emailing that talk show doctor about whether it's healthy for a twelve-year-old boy to wake up to his parents' off-key singing, but so far, he hasn't responded.

"Have a great day, honey," my mom said.

"Yeah, sport," added my dad, before they both shuffled back downstairs. "Come down when you're dressed. I'm making waffles!"

It was hard to stay annoyed when they meant so well.

Hard as it was, though, I was still able to do it.

✦

By the time I got downstairs, Lloyd was there, and he had already eaten most of the waffles.

"Come on!" my dad was shouting. "Do it! Do it!"

My mom rolled her eyes. "Oh, Don, really!"

"Here you go!" Lloyd called, and then he flung a bite of waffle across the room.

My dad practically threw his back out diving for it, but sure enough, he caught it with his front teeth, just like all that broccoli from last night. "Bam!" he cheered. Then he fell over trying to regain his balance and nearly wiped out half the breakfast table with him. Still, his enthusiasm was undimmed. "This needs to be an Olympic event!"

"You'd get the gold, Don," Lloyd assured him.

"One more!" my dad said, brushing himself off. "With my eyes closed!"

"Absolutely not," my mom said, stepping between them. "You can train for the waffle Olympics in somebody else's kitchen. Have a seat, Josh."

My mom snagged the last waffle for me and slid the syrup next to my plate. "How late were you up last night?" she asked.

"Well—" I started to say.

"Not too late, I'm sure," Lloyd interrupted.

"Josh is enjoying his iPhone responsibly. Right, Josh?"

"Of course, Mom."

"I knew you would," she said, bending down and reaching her arms around me for a hug.

From across the room, my mom's phone buzzed. "I wonder who's emailing me," she said.

My dad took his plate to the sink, and Lloyd whispered to me privately, "How did it go last night?"

"Ugh, I'll tell you later."

My mom let out an awful-sounding screech. "Nine hundred dollars!" She tossed down her iPhone.

"Is that the credit card bill?" my dad asked.

"It's the app store bill!" my mom said.

"The wha . . . ?"

"Josh, did you buy nine thousand virtual tickets in a game called *Ultimate* . . ." She looked at the screen, but she couldn't bring herself to say the name. ". . . Something, *Coaster*?"

I froze. I was totally busted. "Doodoofartmama!" I shouted. As soon as it slipped out of my mouth, I realized I shouldn't have said that.

"AAAAAAH!" my mom squealed, as her iPhone fell out of her hands and crashed onto the floor. "Josh!"

My parents are really strict about cursing.[9] They don't want me to say curses, write curses, or even think curses. I would be grounded for a week if I ever said the "s" word ("stupid") or, even worse, the "sh" word ("shut up"). When my dad gets really mad, he yells out "Garbage!" That's the worst word he ever says. One time he got mad while taking out the trash and said, "This garbage is garbage!"

By far, the worst word you can say in my house is definitely the "f" word ("fart"). My mom hates that word. She thinks it's disgusting, even though at Lloyd's

---

9  You can read our blog about curses on page 259. (Just please don't show it to Josh's parents!)

house, it's probably the number one thing anyone says. They're always talking about who farted or whose breath smells like fart or who was born in the fart factory. Even Lloyd's mom says it at dinnertime: "Come and eat, you little farts!" No wonder my mom doesn't like her.

"Josh! How dare you!" my dad said. "Give me your phone, young man!"

I handed him my phone, cringing as he opened the game, a game I had never actually even played.

Lloyd stepped in to rescue me. "Mr. and Mrs. McBain, there have been all kinds of bugs with this new operating system."

"Stay out of this, Lloyd!" my mom snapped. This was very serious if Lloyd's power of persuasion wasn't working.

As my dad tapped his way around Doodoofartmama's messed-up theme park, I heard the music for *Ultimate PukeCoaster* playing, along with the sound of tiny avatars tossing their cookies. "Bleccch!" "A-hoooolph!"

"You spent nine hundred dollars on this?" my dad shouted.

I didn't know what to say. "I'm . . . sorry? I promise. It won't happen again!"

"You're right it won't," my dad said, "because you're not getting this phone back. Not for a month!"

"But, Dad!"

"C'mon, Debbie. We need to leave for work."

As my mom and dad stormed out of the kitchen, I noticed it was only 7:30. "What about quality time?" I asked.

"I'd rather be at work!" my mom shouted.

Every day, my parents made me give them an official Josh Goodbye Hug as they walked out the door. Sometimes I had to pry them off me to get them to leave. Today, though, they just grabbed their coats and pushed past me.

"Excuse me!" my mom said, nudging me aside with her hip.

"Mom . . . ?" I spread my arms out wide for a hug, but by that point, she was halfway down the porch steps.

"We wanted to do something nice for you," she sniffed. "And you took advantage of it!" She looked like she might cry.

I turned toward my dad as he followed her, but he didn't even look at me. He stomped through the doorway, then he stopped himself, as if he'd just remembered something. He doubled back into the kitchen, then came out a moment later tearing up a piece of paper.

"You don't deserve a lunch note today!" he hissed, tossing the ripped-up shreds on the floor.

I'd never seen my parents so angry. I couldn't let them leave like this. This required desperate measures. "I love you!" I called after them. I knew that was the bait they couldn't resist. They'd never not said it back to me.

My dad turned around, and I thought for sure he was going to say it. I could tell from his face, though, that he was in no mood to make peace. "Then you shouldn't have done such . . . such . . ." I could see him debating whether or not to use *the* word. "Such . . . garbage!"

He said it.

Dad climbed into the car and slammed his door, then the Mini Cooper peeled out of our driveway.

I bent down and looked at the lunch note my dad had destroyed. I could tell by reassembling the pieces what it was supposed to say. "Q: Why is your lunch like your iPhone? Because it's loaded with apps!" Next to the word "apps," they'd drawn some apple slices.

It was terrible as always, but I felt a little sad to see

it destroyed by someone other than me. I felt like a bad son—worse, a bad human being.

And it was all the fault of those two slimy space jerks.[10]

---

10   Page 261 has our blog on fights, something Lloyd and I never, ever do. Lloyd thinks it's our best post, but I say he's wrong, and if he disagrees, he's a dopey weasel booger muncher.

# CHAPTER 8

"I've had it!" I shouted when I rejoined Lloyd in the kitchen. "I'm going to kick their butts!"

"Josh," Lloyd replied. I thought he was going to warn me against starting an interplanetary war, but instead, he said, "Remember where their butts are. We both know you can't kick that high."

"I have to do something," I wailed. "My parents hate me!"

"No they don't. They're just filled with rage for right now. Rage fades, trust me."

That was when we heard the buttheads coming downstairs. They were speaking in their native tongue, so loud that their farts nearly shook the walls. Lloyd couldn't help giggling, which only annoyed me more. "Stop it!" I said. "Farts aren't always funny!"

"OK, let me talk to them," Lloyd said. "You're too wound up right now."

I knew Lloyd was the better talker, so I agreed.

"Yo there, Earth friends!" IAmAWeenieBurger chimed as he entered the kitchen. From across the room, he spotted my plate on the table. "Ooh, we've always wanted to try waffles! Do you mind?"

"Help yourselves," Lloyd told them.

IAmAWeenieBurger picked up my plate and placed it on a chair. "Yummy!" he squealed, then he sat down on top of it. I couldn't see exactly what his mouth was doing to the waffle, but I heard ravenous slurping sounds. I had never given any thought to how these aliens eat with mouths where their butts should be, but now that I had the answer, I realized it should've been kind of obvious. I had to admit it was a tiny bit cool, but mostly it was disgusting.

As IAmAWeenieBurger went to town on my breakfast, Doodoofartmama began furiously waving his arms. "FRRT! FRRT!" he blared, and with a mighty shove, he pushed his friend off my chair.

"Whatevs, dude. I'll share." IAmAWeenieBurger

stood back, then Doodoofartmama sat down on what remained of my waffle. He began slurping even louder.

It was only then that I realized there wasn't going to be anything left for me. "Lloyd, that's my breakfast!" I said.

Lloyd tapped Doodoofartmama on the shoulder. "Guys, save some for Josh, OK?"

Doodoofartmama stood up, leaving the shredded remains of my waffle on the chair, drenched in some orange-hued goop that was clearly what buttheads had instead of human spit. "FRRT!" he apologized. His fart sounded sincere, and it had the fresh smell of clean laundry, so I decided not to make a big deal about it. Still, I couldn't bear to look at what was left of my breakfast, let alone eat it.

As I struggled to hold back my barf, IAmAWeenie-Burger proceeded to pick up my orange juice. "Yo! Orange juice!" He bent over so he could pour the juice in his mouth.

I dove for the glass, shouting, "Stooooopppppp!" I couldn't stand to see my OJ disappear into an alien's butt-mouth.

"What? What's wrong?" IAmAWeenieBurger asked.

"You're wrong! Everything about you is wrong!" I shouted.

IAmAWeenieBurger hung his head in the saddest way. "We have flown twenty-three billion light-years to see you. But maybe you don't want us here."

"Frrt," Doodoofartmama concurred, sadly.

"Guys, you are totally welcome on this planet," Lloyd insisted. "Right, Josh?"

"No," I said. "Not until you pay my parents back the nine hundred dollars you spent on iPhone games!"

From between IAmAWeenieBurger's legs, I could see his jaw drop. "Doodoofartmama!" he scolded. "I told you that was a lot of Earth money!" Doodoofartmama frowned guiltily, and IAmAWeenieBurger turned back toward me. "I'm very sorry. We don't have any dollars, but we'll pay you back with ten billion woofbas."

"Whoa!" Lloyd nearly fell over with excitement. "Ten billion? Josh, we'll be rich!"

I rolled my eyes. "The app store doesn't accept woofbas, Lloyd!"

"Right," he said. "Okay, Josh. If this is what you want, we'll kick them out. Thanks for stopping by, buttheads. Don't let the ozone layer hit you on the way out."

The buttheads made super sad faces, and Lloyd glared at me in the hopes I'd feel guilty. But I knew he was up to his usual mind games, and I wasn't falling for it. Not this time. "Keep in touch," I said, coldly.

IAmAWeenieBurger farted sadly at Doodoofartmama, who then farted sadly back. They went on talking this way, and Lloyd shook his head at me, disappointed. "It's not that I feel bad for them," he said. "I feel bad for you, Josh. You deserved better than this."

I was starting to wonder if I was making the right decision. Like I said, Lloyd can be very persuasive, but then I noticed something strange. The buttheads no longer looked sad. They had their backs to us, so I could see their mouths, and while a mouth on a butt is a little different than a mouth on a face, it's still a mouth, and I was pretty sure that theirs were smiling. Not normal smiles, either. Evil smiles. "Um, Lloyd, what do you think they're talking about?"

Lloyd shrugged. "Probably how disappointed they are in our planet."

As I watched them suspiciously, Doodoofartmama suddenly collapsed to the floor in a sickly, stench-ridden blob. *Plop!* He lay there, his eyeballs floating on a pile of goop. It was different from when the aliens went number four, but equally disgusting. Then, suddenly, bubbles appeared, poking up from the surface of the sludge and popping with a little mess of yuckiness.

"What's he doing?" I asked.

IAmAWeenieBurger turned around, nervously. "No worries. He is simply texting our besties."

"That's going to go all the way back to your planet?"

"No, just to a spy satellite that we planted in your orbit ten million butthead years ago. Maybe you've noticed it. Two cheeks, a big crack. We call it the Space Butt."

"That's yours?" I said. "It's not just a fragment from an ancient comet?"

Lloyd nodded proudly. "See, Josh? I really did deserve an A on my report!"

Doodoofartmama burbled on the floor like a pot of spaghetti sauce on the stove. One big bubble over here, then another one over there. Then, he pushed out a bubble the size of my head, and it separated from the rest of his body and began to float upward. It seeped through the window and out of the house, before sailing skyward, up through the clouds, until I couldn't see it anymore.

IAmAWeenieBurger explained. "His butt bubble will let the other buttheads know that we're coming home a little early."

"Oh," I said. "Well, I'm sorry, but that's probably best. Maybe our cultures just don't mix well. No hard feelings."

"Of course not. I am only sad that we will never get to humiliate Quentin for you." Doodoofartmama began to ooze back and forth across the floor and emit sparks.

"What? You were really going to help us defeat Quentin?"

"That is why we came! To help our Earth friends with a noble cause."

"Yeah, Josh," Lloyd said. "They wanted to help us, but if you want them gone . . ."

Now I was flashing an evil smile. I couldn't help it. The thought of getting back at Quentin changed everything. "Well . . . how would you do it?" I asked.

"We would have to figure it out when we got to school."

"School?" I said. "Oh no. We couldn't take you to school[11]."

---

[11] See page 262 for our blog about school, a terrible place to bring aliens— and a pretty miserable place for kids, too.

IAmAWeenieBurger began to cry again, and I ducked to avoid getting soaked.

"It's nothing personal. You're just a little too . . . different."

"Different?"

"Yeah," Lloyd explained. "People tend to notice 'different' in middle school, like if your socks don't match or your backpack has a hole in it, or, maybe, say for example, you have a butt on your head?"

"Well, my butt wouldn't go. Just my eye! We would do an eye swap."

"An eye swap?" I asked. "Is that as gross as it sounds?"

"Here, I'll show you." IAmAWeenieBurger bent down and held his fingerless hand underneath his right eyeball. Then, using his other two hands, he smacked the back of his head really hard. One smack. Two smacks. And then, his eye popped out and rolled onto his open palm.

I nearly fainted. It was the grossest thing I'd ever seen, and only two minutes earlier these weirdos had been sitting on my breakfast.

"Now, you give me yours," IAmAWeenieBurger said. He reached his hands up and whacked me on the back of my head.

"Eek!" I shrieked, backing away. "You're not taking my eyes!"

"Oh, right," he said. "I forgot that's a butthead-only thing. See, we have this cool thing where our eyes, like, transmit images to our brains through phasmic waves."

"What are phasmic waves?" Lloyd asked.

"Oh, right. You humans still haven't discovered phasmic waves." IAmAWeenieBurger laughed mockingly.

"Shut up!" I said. "And you buttheads still haven't invented *Minecraft*."

"Excellent point," IAmAWeenieBurger agreed. "Phasmic waves can, like, beam whatever my eye sees back to my brain, yo. So if you take my eye to school, I'll be able to peep what's happening."

"Well, maybe that works on your planet," I said. "But on Earth, people don't just walk around carrying eyeballs everywhere."

"Wait, Josh," Lloyd said. "This is a great idea. We can hide the eye in your backpack. It can see our school, and nobody has to see it." He grabbed the eyeball from IAmAWeenieBurger's hand. "Here, let's find something to put this in."

With the eyeball in his hand, Lloyd walked into my parents' pantry. IAmAWeenieBurger was standing right next to me, but he could clearly see everything his eyeball was seeing, because he cooed happily, "Whoa, those Oreos look pretty sweet! Ooh, trail mix!"

"Perfect!" Lloyd said. He emerged from the pantry with the eyeball locked up in a Ziploc baggie. "Think fast!" he shouted and tossed the eyeball across the room to me.

I'm not very good at catching things under ideal circumstances, such as when I know someone's about to throw it and when it's not an eyeball. So when Lloyd threw the eyeball at me without warning, I did what I usually do in sports, which is to panic and cover my face, while screaming, "Aah!"

*Thump!* The eyeball fell to the kitchen floor and rolled across the room.

"Oh! I'm getting dizzy!" IAmAWeenieBurger shouted as it spun in the corner.

"Come on, Josh!" Lloyd picked up the baggie and held it out to me. "It's just an eyeball."

I stared at it. It was veiny and curious, looking back at me from inside the bag. Shuddering, I reached out and took it from Lloyd. It gazed all around, taking everything in, as I slid it down into the mesh pocket on the side of my backpack. From there, it would have a pretty good view of my school day—and hopefully, no one would notice it transmitting phasmic waves or whatever.

Just then, Doodoofartmama's butt bubble flew back in through the window and hovered over his sparking goo mound. IAmAWeenieBurger emitted an excited fart as it plopped back down onto his goo pile and was reabsorbed. "Cool!" IAmAWeenieBurger said. "They texted back." Doodoofartmama's body emerged from the sludge and retook its shape.

Lloyd elbowed me, awestruck. "Come on, Josh. You gotta admit it's pretty cool seeing all the crazy stuff they can do."

I wanted to agree with Lloyd, but then, the buttheads started farting at each other again. Whatever Doodoofartmama said to IAmAWeenieBurger made him very happy, and his evil smile came back. Soon, they were both laughing—and looking at us.

"What's so funny?" I asked.

They quickly stopped laughing and tried to act natural. "Nothing," IAmAWeenieBurger said, facing us with only one eye in his skull. "Our friends just texted back a funny joke." They looked at each other and started laughing again. I had no idea what they were saying, but it felt a lot like they were laughing at us.

Lloyd and I shared a suspicious glance. I could tell he was thinking the same thing as me. Something strange was going on, and I was no longer so sure the buttheads had only come to Earth to play video games.

# CHAPTER 9

When I got to homeroom, I wasn't sure what was freaking me out more—the fact that I had an alien's eyeball in my backpack or that at any moment, my parents might show up, desperate to make amends with me. They had never stormed out on me like that before, without a hug or an "I love you, my sweet little pookykins." I could only assume that they were wracked with guilt at how they'd behaved, unable to function. As Mr. Hogan took attendance, I listened to the sounds coming from the hallway, convinced I'd soon hear the *click-clack* of tap shoes. Then, my parents would burst into my classroom, jazz hands waving, in full view of the backpack, to sing me a make-up song. It'd be a new low for me socially, humiliated in front of creatures from two galaxies at once.

While I waited for the inevitable embarrassment, I heard President Quentin come over the loudspeaker. As one of the perks of his office, he got to make the morning announcements, as if the required mumble-through of the Pledge of Allegiance wasn't annoying enough without hearing it led by his nasally voice. "Attention, fellow students," he announced. "This is your president, Quentin Fairchild, speaking, and this is today's State of the School Address." He spoke as if he were the president of the United States telling the public about a war, rather than a student body president announcing a room change for French club.

"I'd like to begin, as always, with a few measured words about an important topic to our school, our generation, and our world. Today's topic: human cloning."

I glanced at Lloyd, wondering if he'd be rolling his eyes as hard as I was. "Some say cloning is playing God. That it's unethical or, worse, dangerous. That we could never anticipate the outcome. I, on the other hand, welcome the prospect. Who knows how the world might benefit from having another Albert Einstein, another Abraham Lincoln, or dare I suggest, another Quentin Fairchild?" He paused, I'm pretty sure because he was expecting his listeners to break out in applause at this point. "Don't we deserve the chance to find out?"

I looked down at my backpack, and I'm pretty sure that from the side pouch, IAmAWeenieBurger was rolling his eyeball, too.

"Brilliant point, Quentin," Principal Hartley interjected. "I think that gives us all something to chew on today."

"Something to chew on." Like Quentin's egotistical tirade was a juicy steak, instead of the rubber turd it really was. Finally, though, Quentin got to the actual announcements.

"I'd like to remind everyone that today after school we'll hold tryouts for the Smart-Off team in the cafeteria. Please inform your homeroom teacher if you'd like to sign up. And if anyone wants to take me on for this year's Super Brain, I welcome the challenge!"

"No, Lloyd," I said, as I say instinctively whenever my best friend has a chance to volunteer me for something. Somehow, though, he was already giving my name to Mr. Hogan. The Smart-Off team was an academic all-star group made up of the biggest nerds in the school in every subject. There was a Science Smarty, a Math Smarty, a Social Studies Smarty, and so on. As I was only maybe the fifth-biggest nerd in any of these areas, I never bothered to try out before.

The Smart-Off team traveled to other schools in the area to compete in quizzes, because some people apparently enjoy tests so much that they're willing to do more of them outside of school. Not me. I knew it was just a lame attempt to turn geekiness into a sport, for people who had pretty much no chance of ever making an actual sports team.

The head of the whole operation was the Smart-Off Super Brain, a position that might as well be called the Super Quentin, because no one was ever going to beat him out for it. I couldn't imagine anyone even bothering to try at this point, except of course for me, because Lloyd was going to make me do it.

He had already crossed the room and got Kaitlyn Wien-Tomita to start filming him. "If you want to see the biggest news story to hit this school all year, come to the Smart-Off tryouts today," he said. "Right, Josh?"

Kaitlyn turned her camera on me, and I had to think fast. "You'll definitely see somebody being humiliated." I smirked.

Kaitlyn turned her camera off. "Thanks for the quotes, guys. This is going to be an awesome story."

"Nah, it's just a boring academic competition," I told her as she packed up her things to go to first period. "Isn't there a soccer game today or a PTA meeting that might be more newsworthy?"

"Don't be modest," Kaitlyn said. "You guys have been so good for me and my channel. That video of Lloyd singing Happy Birthday in fake Japanese has nine hundred hits! I've got new subscribers all the way from Tokyo."

Lloyd watched her go, a proud grin breaking out on his face. "Isn't it great? We're helping launch Kaitlyn's career."

"But, Lloyd," I protested. "I can't take Quentin on for Super Brain. I'll never beat him."

"But what if you did? He'd be devastated! He'd probably cry! It'd be amazing!"

"But it won't happen."

Lloyd grabbed me by the shoulders and looked right into my eyes. "I believe in you, Josh," he said, with such conviction that I almost believed him. "You made aliens come to Earth!"

He was right about that. Contacting extraterrestrials was an accomplishment I could be at least semi-proud of. Still, it wasn't quite relevant. "But I'm terrible at trivia!"

"Dude," Lloyd said. (When he wanted to act really serious, he called me "dude.") "The only way you could let me down is by not even trying."

The bell rang, and for a second I forgot about Quentin and the Smart-Off team. I realized my parents never showed up. Maybe they weren't sorry after all. Maybe they were still disappointed in me. Maybe they'd continue being disappointed in me. This was serious.

I followed Lloyd out to the hallway. "Oh my God," I said. "My parents really don't like me anymore."

"Josh, please. Of course they—" Lloyd stopped himself. "Well, maybe they don't."

"You think so? You think they'll be mad forever?"

"I'm not going to lie, Josh. It could happen." I gasped, devastated. I never realized before how much their opinion actually meant to me. "You'll have to do something big to win them back."

Lloyd stopped walking. It took me a moment to realize why, but when he looked up, I saw what we were standing under, and it made sense. Just over our heads was a banner reading CALLING ALL SMARTIES! SMART-OFF TRYOUTS TODAY!

"If only there was something you could do to impress them," Lloyd said.

I groaned, finally realizing what he was up to. "Fine," I said. "I'll try out." What could go wrong? If I made the team, I'd have something to tell my parents that might take their minds off their iPhone bill. And in the far more likely event that I made a complete fool of myself, at least the only people who'd ever know would be a bunch of kids even nerdier than me.

It turned out IAmAWeenieBurger picked a great day to send his dislodged eyeball to school in my backpack. Mrs. Butler had a mini-meltdown in her lesson on diagramming sentences when no one could remember where to put the preposition. "Here, maybe this will help!" she shouted, and she diagrammed the sentence "I am mad at you" on the Smart Board, and then circled the word "at" like a hundred times. Then, in Social Studies, Mrs. Schapiro did almost her entire lecture on the Bill of Rights without realizing she had a clump of tuna fish on her chin. It wasn't until she got to cruel and unusual punishment that it slid off and landed on Justine Myers's desk, and Justine screamed. And a food fight almost broke out in the cafeteria when Wade Rivers tripped and spilled his gluten-free pepperoni pizza all over Kenneth Booth's limited edition Captain America soccer cleats.

IAmAWeenieBurger seemed to be enjoying it all, but he was especially interested in Mr. Mudd's class. He kept looking around the classroom, his eye darting in all directions. He was checking out the blurry UFO pictures on the bulletin boards, and he was pretty much the only one in class paying attention to Mr. Mudd's extended rant on some supposed top secret government program called Solar Warden, which was supposed to build a fleet of interstellar warships or something. It was during that lecture that I realized we were ignoring a potentially valuable resource.

"Should we ask Mr. Mudd?" I whispered to Lloyd. "About you-know-what?" I motioned toward IAmAWeenieBurger's eyeball in my backpack. "They're up to something."

Lloyd nodded. "Good thinking," he said. "Perfect chance to kiss up to Mudd." It wasn't exactly what I meant, but I was glad he agreed.

"Let's go after school," I said. I knew I couldn't do it now, with IAmAWeenieBurger watching my every move, but I was relieved to know we'd finally get another opinion on the weird alien behavior.

✪

By the end of the day, I'd almost forgotten that before we could talk to Mr. Mudd, we had to go to the Smart-Off tryouts. It was humiliating as soon as I walked into the auditorium. Tryouts were already underway, and Quentin was answering his last question. He was wearing the Smart-Off Super Brain hat, which looks like a giant brain that you wear over your hair, because apparently just being the Super Brain isn't embarrassing enough. They have to make you look ridiculous, too. Just to give himself an extra challenge, he'd chosen to give his answer in Latin.

"Quo qua blah blah blah Marie Curie," he said. Something like that, anyway. As if geek wasn't already enough of a foreign language on its own.

"Brava! Brava!" Principal Hartley cheered. "Brilliant as always!"

When Quentin saw that I had come to tryouts, he didn't say hello or even make some mean-spirited put-down. He just laughed.

"HAHAHAHAHAHAHAHAHAHAHAHAHAHA!"

He laughed so loud and for so long that you would've thought this was the Laugh-Off.

"Ignore him, Josh," Lloyd said.

"I obliterated that test," Quentin said. "A near-perfect score. There's no way you're going to beat me."

Lloyd leaned toward my backpack, where IAmAWeenieBurger's eye sat in a baggie in the side pouch. "In case you were wondering what a donkey-butt jerk looks like," he said, aiming the eye directly at Quentin, "there's the one we've been telling you about."

Kaitlyn Wien-Tomita was there with her camera, and she tried to interview Quentin. "Quentin, can I ask you a few questions about your performance? That was truly amazing!"

"I don't know, Kaitlyn," he said. "How many subscribers do you have?"

Kaitlyn seemed flustered. "Subscribers? Well, I'm kind of just starting, but I got nine hundred views last night, so—

"Call me when you get your first ten million," Quentin sneered. "I don't want to mess up my chance of granting an exclusive interview to the Channel 8 news." Then he leaned right into her lens and added, "I do not grant permission for release of any footage of me in any digital medium, in perpetuity." After that, he blocked his face with his backpack and marched away from her.

Kaitlyn looked distressed, and I could see in her expression that she was going to be a great reporter someday. She had the exact same look on her face that all reporters do when they're in the middle of a story and a pedestrian walks up behind them and jumps up and down, shouting, "Woo-hoo! I'm famous!"

Principal Hartley stood on stage and addressed the two dozen hopefuls seated in front of her. "I assume no one else is trying out for Super Brain, naturally," she said.

"Actually," Lloyd called out, pushing me to the front of the room. "Quentin is about to go down in flames!" Everyone gasped, no one louder than Principal Hartley. Kaitlyn was now filming us as Lloyd shoved me up on stage. "And he'll grant you an exclusive, Kaitlyn. Get ready to meet your new Super Brain, the smartest guy in school, Josh McBain!"

"Um," I stalled. Everyone was staring at me. It seemed like I should say something smart, so I gave it my best shot. "So, like, E equals MC squared!"

"All right, let's get this over with." Principal Hartley sighed. She took a seat and pulled out a sheet of test questions. Kaitlyn followed me with her camera, closing in on my awkward, terrified face. My own principal couldn't even pretend she thought I had a chance, but who could blame her? I was wasting everyone's time here, and we all knew it.

Lloyd leaned in to whisper a final word of advice. "Remember, if you don't know the answer, just make something up. There's always a chance you'll be right." It was pretty much the worst advice ever. There was a one in a million chance a random guess might pay off once . . . but for all twenty questions on the test? The odds were about as good as me winning the lottery every day for a month while simultaneously being attacked by wild badgers.

Principal Hartley handed me the Super Brain hat, and I tried not to vomit or die from embarrassment as I put it on. I took my seat at the front of the cafeteria, and every eye in the room was on me, including IAmAWeenieBurger's eye. Lloyd was holding my backpack for me, making sure the eye was pointed right at me at all times. Talk about pressure!

"Question one," Principal Hartley said. "Math." What a relief! Math was my best subject. "Name every prime number whose square root is an integer."

She looked at me, along with everyone else, and the room fell totally silent. I could hear the clock ticking.

I'm not sure exactly how long the silence lasted, but I'd guess it was somewhere between five seconds and five years.

"I'll need an answer," Principal Hartley insisted.

I took a deep breath as the words swirled in my head. "Prime number . . ." "square root . . ." "integer . . ." I knew what those terms meant on their own, but when you put them all together like that, it was like another language.

I needed more time. "Just one . . ." I started to say, but I couldn't even come up with the next word of my request. One second? One moment?

"Correct!" Principal Hartley replied, sounding shocked. "One is the only prime number whose square root is an integer."

Lloyd pumped his fist and gave me a thumbs-up. Quentin rolled his eyes and muttered under his breath, "Easy." It felt so good to get one right, even if it was a complete accident. Maybe I could quit now. I wouldn't win, but at least I'd end with a perfect 100 percent on the questions I'd been asked so far.

"Question two," Principal Hartley read, "History." I gulped. History was my worst subject. I knew that important things happened in 1492 and 1776, but that was pretty much it. "Who was the first natural-born US president?"

Natural-born? What did that even mean? Were some of our presidents hatched? Well, at least there were a limited number of possible answers. All I had to do was name a president, and I'd have a one-in-however-many-presidents-there-have-been chance of being right.

Who was I kidding? I could only name about five presidents without looking them up. George Washington. Abraham Lincoln. I knew there were two Roosevelts . . . Franklin and . . . Bobby? Justin? No, Justin Roosevelt was a kid in my karate class when I was nine. Man, I couldn't even think of the second Roosevelt's name. All right, so I wouldn't guess him.

"Time's running out, Mr. McBain," Principal Hartley warned.

I had to say something. Lincoln seemed like a good guess. It probably wasn't right, but at least I knew for sure he was a president, so I wouldn't look too dumb. I glanced back at Lloyd, and this time, I made contact with IAmAWeenieBurger's eyeball. I stared deeply at it and decided to shout Lincoln as confidently as I could.

"Martin Van Buren!" I said. What? Where did that come from? I had forgotten all about that guy. Why would I have called out his name instead of the one I was actually thinking?

I could tell from the stunned look on Quentin's face that I got it right. Principal Hartley was so shocked she double-checked her answer sheet. "Um . . . yes!" she announced.

"Really!" I said. "Are you sure?" Lloyd pumped his fist in excitement, while Quentin sat forward in his seat, skeptically. Seeing the pride on Lloyd's face felt good, but even better was the annoyance on Quentin's. He scowled at me, with his arms folded across his chest, daring me to keep my winning streak going.

I couldn't explain it, but I wasn't going to argue with a correct answer. Maybe I was smarter than I thought.

"Question three. Grammar. Answering this question is easy. Just name what part of speech the word 'answering' is in the previous sentence."

This time, I didn't even hesitate. "A gerund!" I announced, clearly and confidently.

"Correct!" Principal Hartley cheered. She shot me a huge smile. "Very impressive, Mr. McBain."

Lloyd was practically doing a jig around Quentin's chair. He was so excited—and Quentin was so annoyed. But I had a nagging feeling that something was wrong.

For starters, I had never heard the word "gerund" before in my life. That's a part of speech? We never studied that in class. How could I possibly have known that was the answer?

I felt bad for a second or two, and then I felt great again, because getting answers right was awesome, and it was more fun to focus on that feeling than the guilt or confusion.

"Question four. Astronomy. Which planet has the most moons?"

Once again, the answer came to me in a flash. "The planet with the most moons is X4-Furg88 in the Galbutron galaxy, with 9,487."

The room was silent. What did I just say? Suddenly, I realized where the answers were coming from. I gazed at my backpack, and I saw the eye trained right on my brain.

"IAmAWeenieBurger!" I shouted.

Principal Hartley seemed flustered. She flipped through the answer sheet. "Well, a weenie burger wouldn't have gotten those first three questions right. But if you're saying you want to change your answer for this one, you have ten seconds left."

I forced out a chuckle. "I was just kidding! You mean

this solar system, right?" I looked back at the eye, and it seemed to beam the answer directly to me. "Obviously, that would be Jupiter, with sixty-three discovered so far by lackluster Earth astronomers."

Principal Hartley checked her answer sheet. "Correct!"

I felt queasy. I had never cheated on a test before. My conscience told me to stop, but everything else was telling me to keep going. The shock on Quentin's face. The pride on Lloyd's. The thought of telling my parents I'd won. And, of course, the severed eyeball that was helping me cheat. The aliens were an advanced race, after all. Who was I to argue with them on what was the right thing to do?

I didn't get a single question wrong for the rest of the quiz. Not only that, I answered them in record time. I even answered Principal Hartley when she said, "Aren't you just the smartest kid in school?" with an unqualified, "Yes!" Quentin went through a range of emotions. At one point, he just sat there frozen, with his jaw hanging open. Later, he became a whimpering mess. But when Principal Hartley announced that I would be the new Super Brain, his expression changed instantly.

He was furious.

Everyone in the room stood up and cheered for me. Kaitlyn came racing up with her camera for a close-up. Quentin was so enraged he cut her off before she got to me. "I'd like to say a few words on the record," he hissed.

"Sorry," Kaitlyn said, weaving around him. "I want to talk to the winner. Josh, how did you do it?"

I waited for another perfect answer to nuzzle its way into my brain, but this time, IAmAWeenieBurger left me on my own, with the blinking light of the camera petrifying me into stupidity. "Well, me do good smart answers," was all that came out.

Thankfully, Principal Hartley rescued me from the awkward moment. She stood up and enthusiastically shook my hand. "I never knew there was anyone in our school as smart as Quentin," she gushed. "Let alone someone even smarter! Perhaps we should call you Josh Mc*Brain*!"

Quentin was a bit less noble about my victory. "Wow, congratulations, Josh," he said. "It's almost as if you had a copy of the test in advance." Now, Kaitlyn pointed her camera at him, but he was too absorbed to realize his meltdown was being caught on video.

"Sorry, Quentin," Lloyd said. "Josh won fair and square. Now we all know who the real Super Brain is around here."

"Impossible!" Quentin spat. "No one's smarter than me! I know you cheated. Cheater! CHEATER!" He shouted as loudly as he could, but everyone else mostly ignored him. His face grew red with fury, and a huge vein started bulging out on his forehead. Snarling like a bull, he jumped up on a table and stomped his foot to get people's attention. "This Super Brain competition has been tainted by LIES! Josh cheated, and I'm going to find out how!"

"Good luck," Lloyd said, leading me out of the room. "Too bad you've been having so much trouble coming up with answers today."

Lloyd and I hurried away triumphantly, but we made sure that as we left, we laughed loud enough for Quentin to hear.

"HAHAHAHAHAHAHAHAHAHAHAHAHA!"

I could tell from the look on Kaitlyn's face that she thought this was going to be another kick-butt video.

# CHAPTER 10

The celebration for my victory lasted about five minutes, and then Lloyd reminded me that we were supposed to talk to Mr. Mudd. Of course, before we could have that conversation, I had to lie to an eyeball. "That was really amazing how you helped me become the Smart-Off Super Brain," I whispered into the mesh pocket of my backpack as I shoved it into my locker. "But now, I have to . . . um . . ." I looked to Lloyd for help, and as usual, he knew just what to say.

"He's gonna make a celebratory poop. Earth tradition." It's hard to tell whether IAmAWeenieBurger believed him, because his eye couldn't actually respond, but we had to get to Mr. Mudd's room before he left for the day. So I slammed the locker door shut, then

Lloyd and I hurried down the hallway. "Let me do all the talking," Lloyd said. As if there was any question.

It was half an hour after school ended, so my heart sank when I saw the lights in his classroom were off. "Maybe we can catch him in the parking lot," I said.

Lloyd shook his head. "No, this is what he does. Come on." He waved me over to the door, and we peeked in the window to see what was going on.

Mr. Mudd was there, all right. The lower half of his body was bent over the radiator near the windows. The top half of his body was buried underneath the shades, moving around in a regular pattern. "What's he doing?"

Lloyd reached for the doorknob as he explained. "You ever see those flashes of light across the soccer field around this time of day? I think this is where they come from."

We slowly opened the door and let ourselves into Mr. Mudd's room. Before doing whatever he was apparently doing now, he must've been eating. There was a nearly finished burrito, a big bowl of chili fries, and two cans of Mountain Dew on his desk. I had a feeling he wouldn't have wanted us to see any of this, but Lloyd didn't seem concerned.

It's weird to walk up behind somebody who has no idea you're there. I wasn't sure what to say to let him know we'd entered the room. As it turned out, he was the one to make the first sound.

*FRRRRRRRRT!*

Yes, my teacher farted, with Lloyd and me just a few feet away. It seemed like a good reason to retreat quickly to the hallway, but before I could, there was another sound . . .

Lloyd laughing. Loudly.

"HEH-HEH-HEH-HEH-HEH!"

The next thing I knew, there was a blinding light in my face, as the window shade shot up and flapped around the roller with a sound as loud as a machine gun. *BAP! BAP! BAP!* It took a moment for my eyes to focus and see that Mr. Mudd was holding a reflecting board covered in a hundred tiny mirrors. It was bouncing sunlight off every surface in the room, right into my face. "I knew you'd come!" he shouted.

Once I was able to focus, I saw Mr. Mudd looking stranger than he ever had before. He was wearing a face mask with green-tinted goggles and a hat made from tinfoil. He looked almost like an alien himself.

Apparently, it was around then that Mr. Mudd was

able to focus as well. "Boys!" he said. He stashed his mirror board on a shelf and ripped his face mask off. "I thought you were them!"

"Them?" I said.

"You know . . ." Mr. Mudd pointed out the window, up to the sky. "Them!"

"Right," Lloyd said.

"You probably think I'm crazy," Mr. Mudd sighed.

"Not at all!" Lloyd said. "In fact, we have some questions. About 'them.'"

"You do?" Mr. Mudd said. "Really? You want to talk about aliens?" He had this huge smile on his face, the way my two-year-old cousin gets when I agree to play trains with him. "Have a seat! Tell me. Have you met aliens? Seen a UFO? Received telepathic brainwaves from beyond?"

"Uh, none of those," I explained. "We're just curious."

"I see," Mr. Mudd responded, disappointed. "What do you want to know?"

"Well, you always talk about how dangerous aliens would be, how they're spying on us, how they'd want to take over or blow up the Earth for fun. But Earth's a pretty cool planet, right?" Lloyd said. "So we were just wondering if maybe you have it wrong. Maybe aliens would come here just to, like, hang out."

"You fool!" Mr. Mudd exploded. Then, he caught his breath and calmed himself down. "Sorry, boys. Maybe I got a little carried away just now."

"Yeah, kinda," I replied. "I think Lloyd has a point."

"FOOL!" Mr. Mudd shouted again. Then again, he calmed himself down. "Sorry. Boys, let me explain something. This planet we live on is a one-in-a-universe kind of gold mine. Breathable air, plenty of water, a livable climate. If aliens are exploring space, it's because they're looking for those things. They want what we have, and in all likelihood, they have the means to get it, so we're all doomed! DOOMED!" For the third time, Mr. Mudd had become so worked up that he had to stop and catch his breath.

"Oxygen is nice," Lloyd said. "But so are video games, right?"

"Video games?" Mr. Mudd repeated. When he heard those two words, his entire expression changed. It was like we had said the magic words. "Are you sure you haven't met any aliens?"

"Positive," I said. I pulled on Lloyd's shirt and started to back up toward the doorway. Something about Mr.

Mudd's face got me very nervous. "We should probably go."

"Listen, boys," Mr. Mudd continued. "Even if aliens say their intentions are innocent, they shouldn't be trusted. All it would take is one provocation and they might choose to invade. Be vigilant. Always be vigilant!" He yanked the window shade down, plunging the room back into darkness. Lloyd and I got out of there as fast as we could.

Once we were in the hallway, I could see that Lloyd was just as concerned as I was. "Did you see how he got when I mentioned video games?" Lloyd asked.

I nodded. "Oh my God, Lloyd," I said, just having a revelation. "That explains his food. Burritos, chili fries, soda. He meant to fart like that."

"What?"

"He was shining a light at the sky and farting. He was talking to them!"

"Whoa, maybe he does know what he's talking about," Lloyd said. "Maybe those buttheads aren't so nice after all."

I looked at my watch. "We'd better get IAmAWeenieBurger's eyeball out of my locker before he gets suspicious."

Lloyd followed me back to my locker. We were in such a hurry that we didn't even see that someone had been standing outside Mr. Mudd's door the whole time, listening to our conversation.

# CHAPTER 11

Until we knew for sure what the aliens were up to, Lloyd and I decided we should at least pretend that everything was fine. As we walked home, we kept thanking IAmAWeenieBurger's eyeball for his help in defeating Quentin. "You did it!" I shouted. "Quentin was so furious!"

"Buttheads rule!" Lloyd agreed.

I could barely believe it happened. We won. Quentin couldn't mock us or look down on us anymore, because I'd beaten him out for the Super Brain. Maybe this was a new beginning for me. Maybe I could be successful like he was, appreciated and adored. Unfortunately, my joy lasted only until we got back to my house. That's when two things went horribly wrong. First, we saw what the aliens did to the place while I was gone all day. The whole house was a mess. There was toilet paper running up and down the hall. My video games were scattered around the living room. And worst of all, there was a giant puddle of barf on the floor that seemed to be made up mostly of Oreo chunks. The aliens were lying next to it, sound asleep, and there was something else very strange about them.

They were enormous.

While we were in school, they got fat. Like, super fat. Twice as big as they were before. As with humans, most of the weight went to their butts, but since their butts were on their heads, that was going to make it nearly impossible for them to stand up.

"Whoa, what happened here?" I asked, nudging IAmAWeenieBurger with my foot.

IAmAWeenieBurger rolled over and opened his one remaining eye for a look around the room. "What's the prob? Everything's cool."

I tossed him my backpack, and he fished his eyeball out of the pocket. As soon as he popped it back in its socket, he cringed at what he could now see. "Oh wait, never mind," he said. "Yikes."

It was then that I noticed an empty bottle a few feet

away from them. "No!" I shouted. "That's not . . ." I tip-toed past the aliens so I wouldn't get Oreo barf on my sneakers. Then, I picked up the bottle, confirming my worst fear. "You drank the Quokka Kola?"

Doodoofartmama rolled over, holding his head, one hand on each butt cheek and the third on his fore-head. "FRRT!" (The sound was as uncomfortable as the smell, which reminded me of a wet Band-Aid.)

"Yeah, my head hurts, too," IAmAWeenieBurger said.

"Josh," Lloyd said calmly, "don't freak out. It's just a soda."

"Just a soda! My dad got this in Australia!"

"I thought your dad never did anything cool."

"It wasn't cool. It was a work trip when my mom was pregnant with me. He didn't get to throw a boo-merang or wrestle a crocodile or do anything fun. He got sent to a tiny town called Goonscrudger's Gully. It was known for being the place kangaroos went to die. All day long he'd look out the window and see them hopping slowly down the street. And worst of all, they had no Wi-Fi!"

"Whoa!" Lloyd was horrified.

"Then he got bitten by a wallaby and came down

with this rare marsupial flu, and the State Department wouldn't let him come home for a month. He missed my birth because of it. The only thing he enjoyed while he was there was this local drink he discovered. Quokka Kola. So when he finally got to leave, he kept one bottle and promised to save it for the most special of special days."

Lloyd shrugged and slurped up what was left in the bottle. "Eh, tastes like Pepsi."

"Lloyd!"

"What? We can just fill the bottle with some other soda. He'll never know. If I were you, I'd be more worried about these barfed-up Oreos."

"Semi-barfed-up," IAmAWeenieBurger corrected. The two aliens rubbed their eyes and rolled over. "We were totally gonna finish them."

Doodoofartmama positioned his mouth over the puddle and started lapping it up with his tongue.

"Eww!"

"What do you humans do when you eat something really delish?" IAmAWeenieBurger asked. "Maybe thank the chef and eat some more? Well, we barf it back up! Then we eat it again. Then we barf it, then we eat it. Barf it, eat it. Barf it, eat it. Until all the flavor's gone. You can tell how much we like something by how many times we blow chunks."

Lloyd approached them. "I'm glad you like Oreos, but I think they may have caused you to put on a bit of weight."

IAmAWeenieBurger tried to sit up, but his enormous butt kept causing him to fall back over. His head on the ground, he held the bag of Oreos up to his face so he could read it. "I suspect it has something to do with your strange Earth ingredients." He scanned through the label. "Sugar. High-fructose corn syrup. Mmmm . . . soy lecithin!"

"Just clean it up, please." I went to the kitchen, and what I saw there was an even bigger mess. There were food crumbs everywhere, and the inside of the microwave was coated in a weird brown goo. "What did you put in the microwave?"

"I'm not sure what they're called," IAmAWeenieBurger replied, "but we found them oozing around in the garden."

I took a closer look and saw tiny eyeballs and antennae floating in the gunk. "You put slugs in the microwave?"

"Well, you didn't expect us to eat them raw, did you?"

As I was wondering whether I wanted to be known as the first human to strangle an alien, Lloyd stepped in and took charge. "OK, we have approximately fifty-three minutes before Josh's parents get home. We need to clean everything up."

This was the great thing about Lloyd. He always kept his cool in a crisis, and he always had a plan. I cleaned the microwave while the aliens licked up the mess on the floor. As for the Australian soda, Lloyd refilled the bottle with some supermarket brand diet cola. Then, all that was left was for the aliens to lap up the last of their barf.

"Finally," I sighed. "Now we can relax!"

I went to sit on the couch, but just as I was plopping down, IAmAWeenieBurger shouted, "Wait! Not there!"

It was too late. My butt rammed against the hard bottom of the sofa, shooting pain up my back. "Ow!" I looked down, and underneath me was a completely flat couch cushion. "What happened to the stuffing?" I groaned.

"FRRT!" Doodoofartmama said, and a puffy white cloud shot out of his mouth.

"It was delicious!" IAmAWeenieBurger agreed. "We barfed that up nine times!"

Once again, Lloyd swooped in before I did the aliens

any bodily harm. "We're going to need something soft to fill those up again. I've got it!"

I followed him into my parents' bedroom, but once I saw what he was looking at, I shook my head. "No, Lloyd! We can't use those!"

We were standing in front of the Great Undershirt Mountain. My dad had so many undershirts that he hardly ever had to wash them. At the end of every day, he just tossed the dirty one on top of the pile. He only washed them when he ran out of undershirts in his drawer, usually once every six months or so.

"He'll never notice a few of them missing," Lloyd said. He held his nose with one hand and started picking up sweat-stained undershirts with the other.

The cushions were a little lumpy when we were done refilling them, but as Lloyd pointed out, they were softer than ever, and after a few seconds, you barely noticed the smell.

"Look at that!" he said proudly. "With ten minutes to spare!"

Unfortunately, just as I was about to thank Lloyd for fixing everything, that's when the second horrible thing happened that ruined our day. All of a sudden, Doodoofartmama began running in circles, waving his arms like a maniac and farting his head off. Something was majorly freaking him out.

I asked IAmAWeenieBurger to translate. "Hmmm . . ." he said. "You might want to pull the curtains. He says there's somebody looking at us."

"What?"

I ran up to the window and scanned the backyard. There, sitting in a tree, I saw someone watching us through a pair of binoculars.

"There really is someone!" I waved Lloyd over to look.

"Well . . ." IAmAWeenieBurger said. "Who could it be?" He peeked over my shoulder, in full view of the window.

"Get away!" I screamed. "He'll see you!" That's when I realized who the spy was, because as I was frantically trying to shove IAmAWeenieBurger out of sight, the person in the bushes put down his binoculars and took out his phone.

"Oh, it's him!" IAmAWeenieBurger said, as we both got a glimpse of Quentin fumbling to take a picture[12]. "Hmmm . . . that's bad."

---

12   See page 264 for our blog on taking pictures, humanity's number one most worthless pastime.

I pulled the curtains, but I knew it was too late. Quentin had seen IAmAWeenieBurger. He may even have snapped a photo of him. "We have to stop him!" I said.

Lloyd ran for the back door. "Don't worry. I'll fix this."

It was a relief to hear Lloyd sounding so confident. Lloyd never let me down. By the time I got to the back door, I could see he was already working things out with Quentin.

"That's right," Lloyd told him. "There are aliens in Josh's house. They saw our website, and they came to meet us, and they have butts in the back of their heads."

"Lloyd!" I wailed. I couldn't believe he was confessing everything.

"We can't lie anymore, Josh," he said. "It's true, Quentin. They sleep in Josh's bed, they play video games, and they eat couch stuffing."

"I knew it!" Quentin shouted. Then he added, "I mean, not the couch stuffing. That's kinda weird."

"Isn't it?" Lloyd agreed.

Quentin stepped forward accusingly. "And they helped Josh cheat at the Smart-Off tryouts, didn't they?"

"That's right," Lloyd said. "They mentally beamed

him every answer through an eyeball in Josh's backpack."

"Lloyd, stop!" I begged. Lloyd turned toward me and winked. I wasn't sure what he was up to, but I could see it was all part of his plan.

"Where are they?" Quentin demanded. "I want to see them."

"Just look through the window." Lloyd pointed toward the house. "And stay still so they can get a good shot at you."

"Shot?" Quentin repeated.

"Well, I'm sure they have their Ultra BrainSuck 3000 pointed at you right now."

"They're going to k-k-kill me?" Quentin shuddered.

"Kill you? No, that would be ridiculous, to destroy a perfectly developed human brain like yours."

"Oh," Quentin sighed in relief.

"They're just going to steal your mental function."

"Wh-wh-what?" Quentin stumbled backward nervously.

"Not all of it, of course. Just the genius parts. You'll still be able to live a perfectly normal life as someone with average intelligence."

"No!" Quentin wailed. I'd never seen him so terrified.

I had to smile. Seeing Lloyd manipulate people was like watching a master at work. I just still wasn't sure exactly what his plan was.

"Average people lead wonderful lives," Lloyd assured him with false sincerity. "Think of the possibilities. You could go on to be a cashier . . . or a sewage treatment technician . . . or maybe even a teacher!"

"NOOOOOOOOOO!" Quentin took off running, covering his head in case an alien ray beam came shooting at him.

Lloyd laughed hysterically. "Lloyd, you let him get away!" I shouted.

"So what? He's terrified they'll steal his brain. And even if he does tell people, they'll never believe him."

"But, Lloyd," I said. "They might believe him if he has a picture."

"Wait." Lloyd froze. "He took a picture?"

I nodded. "I'm pretty sure he did. Now the whole world is going to know about the buttheads! They'll wrap our houses in plastic and hook us up to machines that never stop beeping. You saw *E.T.*!"

"Yeah, that was a good movie."

"Lloyd, we invited them to our planet to have fun, and now they're just going be guinea pigs. We'd better hope there's no Yelp in outer space, because they will not say nice things about us."

"You're right," Lloyd said. "Let me think."

In all the years I had known Lloyd, I had never seen him think before.

It wasn't pretty. But a minute later, he had the answer. "It's time, Josh," he said, taking a deep breath. "The buttheads need to go home."

# CHAPTER 12

"I'm really sorry, dude," Lloyd told me as we walked inside to tell the buttheads to beat it. "I know you've loved having aliens stay in your house."

"Are you mental?" I said. "They got my iPhone taken away. They sat on my waffles. They overwrote my save files. They barfed all over the living room."

"Yeah, they're pretty cool," Lloyd said, not getting it at all.

I checked my laptop and saw that Quentin had already posted his picture on Instagram. It was blurry and taken from far away, but in it, you could see a buttheaded weirdo through the window of my parents' living room.

"Come on, Josh," Lloyd told me. "Let's break the news to them."

I folded up my laptop and tucked it under my arm. Of course, when we got to the living room, IAmAWeenieBurger and Doodoofartmama were on their best behavior. The floor was spotless. The only traces of Oreo barf left were around the corners of their mouths. "Look, guys!" IAmAWeenieBurger called out. "We cleaned!"

"That's great, guys," Lloyd said. "But I'm afraid Josh has some bad news. Go ahead, Josh."

I couldn't believe Lloyd was making me lower the boom. I decided the easiest thing to do was just to show them the picture. "Quentin just posted this online," I said. I opened my laptop and let them see.

IAmAWeenieBurger gasped. "That's Doodoofartmama!"

"I know," Lloyd said. "And it's not even a very flattering angle of him."

"Now everyone will know about us! All of Earth will learn we are here!"

Lloyd and I shared nervous glances. "Yeah, so it's really not safe here for you anymore."

"You are right," IAmAWeenieBurger agreed. "There is

only one thing we can do." He turned to Doodoofartmama and had a short exchange in fart talk, after which Doodoofartmama nodded. Then Doodoofartmama made himself into a blob and started bubbling up.

He was sending another text.

We watched the bubble separate from the rest of the filthy ooze heap and float upward out the window. "I'm sorry," Lloyd said to them. "We wish you guys could stay longer."

"Stay?" IAmAWeenieBurger smiled. "Well, of course we're going to stay!"

"I thought he was texting them that you're coming back early," I said.

IAmAWeenieBurger laughed. "No, he's texting them to come!"

"What?"

Before he could explain, I heard a sound that stopped me cold. It was actually two sounds mixed together, that of a tiny car engine chugging down the street and of a middle-aged man and woman shout-singing, "We built this city on rock and roll!"

"My parents are home!"

I said it thinking the buttheads would take the hint to run upstairs and hide, but instead IAmAWeenieBurger started wobbling his way toward the front door. "Great!" he said. "I'll be delighted to finally meet them!"

"Lloyd, help!" I begged as the Mini Cooper idled in the driveway.

"Don't worry, Josh," Lloyd assured me. "The four of us need to talk this out. Until then, everyone who wasn't born on Earth needs to just hang out in Josh's room for a few minutes. Okay?"

IAmAWeenieBurger turned around. "Well, I'll need some help getting up the stairs." He looked down at the ground, where Doodoofartmama was still nothing but a pile of slime. "And he'll need a lot of help."

My parents got out of the car. We only had a few seconds left. "Josh, you help him, and I'll take care of Doodoofartmama."

For a second, I thought I got the easier job, until I realized how hard it is for an alien with an enormous butt to make it up a staircase. Grabbing an alien's butt was probably the second to last thing on Earth I wanted to do at that moment. But since getting caught by my parents was the absolute last thing I wanted to do, I reached down and wedged my hands under IAmAWeenieBurger's flabby cheeks, lifting with all my might. Ugh!

I could hear my dad turning his key in the front door, so I pushed the alien to the stairs as fast as I could. "Hurry!" I whispered in his ear. "We're almost there."

Meanwhile, Lloyd struggled behind us with his hands full of Doodoofartmama goo. Thankfully, the bubble transmission alien gunk wasn't as sticky as the number four gunk, so the living room stayed pretty clean. It was very gooey, though, like rotten brownie batter or lumpy spoiled milk. Lloyd had to keep shifting his arms around to keep dribbles of Doodoofartmama from plopping to the floor. "Hurry, Josh!" he commanded.

My heart was racing. The front door began to open, and I shoved IAmAWeenieBurger with all my might down the hallway. "Ow!" he whimpered as he stumbled into my bedroom.

Downstairs, my parents began looking around for me. "Josh?" my dad said.

"Lloyd, hurry!" I whispered. He just had to get that massive glob of alien life into my bedroom before my parents saw it. "Throw him!"

Lloyd took a deep breath and did just that, heaving the mound of extraterrestrial slop toward my doorway. It seemed to fly in slow motion through the air. My eyes darted back and forth between it and my clueless parents, wondering if it would sail out of sight before they happened to look its way.

I ran to my bedroom door and waited. As soon as Doodoofartmama flew past, I slammed it shut, but not before I noticed the sludge landing right on top of IAmAWeenieBurger. "Ohhhhhh!" he groaned. Then, as I turned away and breathed a sigh of relief, I heard him from behind the closed door utter a soft, satisfied, "Yummy!"

"Josh?" my parents said, looking up at me and Lloyd.

We had made it, with literally a second to spare. We turned around and tried to play it cool. "Oh, hey," I said. "What's up?"

"Well, hello, Don and Debbie!" Lloyd chimed in, giving a feeble wave.

My parents shared a concerned look. "What's that all over you?" my mom asked.

It was only then that I realized that Lloyd was drenched in whatever Doodoofartmama turned into when he sent text messages.

"We were doing a science experiment," Lloyd said. "Extra credit, for school. Right, Josh?"

"Yeah," I agreed. When in doubt, I've learned, always play along with Lloyd.

"I wanted to goof off and play video games, but your son is very dedicated to his studies!"

My mom and dad looked at each other silently for a moment. I was sure we were busted this time.

"Boys, come down to the living room, please," my mom said, finally. "Your father and I want to apologize for our behavior this morning."

Apologize? So that was what was going on? Lloyd patted me on the back, and I was filled with the pride that comes from getting away with something. I couldn't help smiling. I had tricked my parents. This must be how Lloyd felt, every single day. It was such a rush.

Lloyd and I followed my parents into the living room and sat down across from them on the sofa. My dad put his hand on his left temple and shook his head. "We acted like garbage," he said.

"Don!" my mom said, shocked.

"No, there's no other word for it. Son, Lloyd, I'm sorry."

"We love you so much, honey," my mom said, leaning in for a hug, "even if you did one bad thing."

When I turned ten, I decided I was too big to cry, and I vowed never to do it again. Since then, there have only been two and a half occasions when I absolutely couldn't avoid it. Once was in gym class when Kenny Ferris hit me full speed in the junk with a dodgeball. Once was when Mufasa died in *The Lion King*. And lastly, just a little bit, was when I realized at that moment that my parents still loved me. (No tears actually came out, so that's why I only counted it as a half.) I couldn't speak, because I was afraid I'd start blubbering like a baby. Besides, I didn't know what to say. Thankfully, Lloyd stepped in to make things right.

"We forgive you," he said, pulling us all in for a group hug. "Even the best parents make mistakes."

As we all embraced, I saw Doodoofartmama's butt bubble pulsing back in through the window. It was floating around, as if confused that the rest of the goo was no longer where it expected it to be.

"Lloyd!" I whispered, swatting at it with my hands.

"On it, Josh," he said. He slipped away from the hug and grabbed the bubble with both hands. Then, he served it like a volleyball straight up the stairs and into my bedroom, where it seeped through the door. It was the most athletic thing either of us had ever done, at just the time when we needed it most.

As the hug finally came to an end, Lloyd addressed

my parents. "Now that that's out of the way," he said, "Josh has some big news!"

"Really?" my mom said.

I stood up, proudly, and smiled. "I kind of became the Smart-Off Super Brain today."

My dad gasped. "Did something happen to Quentin? Did he die?"

"No!" I said. "I beat him! I got the highest score on the quiz!"

"Really?" my mom said. "I mean, honey, that's amazing!"

"That's my son!" my dad shouted. I'd never seen him so proud of me. "This calls for a celebration!"

"A special celebration!" my mom said.

"Are you thinking what I'm thinking?" my dad asked.

My mom nodded. "It's time to drink that special soda!"

I nearly screamed.

In an instant, all the joy and relief I'd been feeling transformed into utter terror. I nudged Lloyd, hoping he could come up with a way out of this. He sprang into action, pleading with my parents not to open the bottle.

"No! It's so old! It's probably gone flat. This isn't special. What are you going to drink when Josh gets married? Dr. Pepper?"

Nothing worked. My dad pulled out the bottle and four small glasses, then began to pour. "Josh, you make me so proud. The only way to do this moment justice is with some Quokka Kola."

He raised his glass to toast, and we all clinked. I watched my dad close his eyes and smile in anticipation. He held the soda underneath his nose like he was taking in the bouquet of a fine wine. Then, he held the glass to his lips and ever so gently took his first loving sip.

Which he promptly spat out in disgust, right in my mom's face.

"Aah!" she screamed, as the cut-rate cola shot directly up her left nostril.

"This is the supermarket brand!" He turned to me and Lloyd, his face bright red with rage.

"Did you boys break into my soda stash?"

"No, Dad!" I said.

"The label is wet. Someone opened this today."

"We didn't do it!" Lloyd said.

"Don't give me that . . ." my dad replied, pausing

as he pondered what to say next. I'd never seen him so angry, not even that morning.

"Don, no!" my mom said. She was shaking her head, gushing tears of disappointment. "Don't say it."

"GARBAGE!!!" my dad exploded. "That's what it is! It's garbage! It's DARN garbage! And after we said we were sorry!"

"Don," Lloyd said, trying to stay calm. "Mr. McBain, please let me explain."

"Lloyd, go home!" my dad shouted.

"Yes, sir," Lloyd replied, running for the door. When Lloyd abandons ship, you know you're in trouble.

Then, my dad turned to me. "Joshua James McBain, the third," he said, "You are grounded! You are not allowed to leave your room except for school, from now until the end of time!"[13]

I wanted to defend myself, but I could tell from the look on his face that I'd never win this battle. "I understand," I said, backing away with my head hung low. I was hoping he'd say something else to me as I walked upstairs, one final statement to let me know that, as enraged as he was, he still loved me.

---

13 See page 266 for our blog on punishments, which are parents' revenge whenever a kid does something cool.

"Young man," he said, as I reached the top of the stairs.

"Yes, Dad?" I said hopefully.

"I'm very disappointed in you."

It was then that my second-and-a-half time crying became an official number three.

# CHAPTER 13

I was so upset about disappointing my parents that I forgot for a moment that more aliens were on their way to our planet and that all of Earth could soon be bathed in number four and Oreo barf. All I could do was hope this was a misunderstanding that I could quickly clear up with the buttheads.

As I approached my bedroom, though, things didn't sound so simple. There was a lot of farting coming from the other side of the door, and a lot of evil laughs, too. I decided to eavesdrop for a minute, so I quietly pushed the door open a crack and began to observe.

The buttheads looked normal again—well, normal for them, at least. They'd reformed from their jellylike state, and they'd returned themselves to their usual proportions. The butt cheeks bulging out of their craniums were back to the size and shape I remembered.

It wasn't their appearance that stood out the most, though. It was what they were doing—bent over my globe with a red Sharpie.

"FRRT FRRT FRRT Paris?" IAmAWeenieBurger asked.

"FRRT!" Doodoofartmama agreed eagerly. Then, IAmAWeenieBurger drew a giant *X* over half of France.

With every successive fart, the room filled more and more with the smell of raw beef. It was like the butcher counter at the supermarket.

That couldn't be a good sign.

There were *X*'s all over the globe, as it turned out—dozens of them, everywhere from Wagga Wagga, Australia, to Walla Walla, Washington. This was exactly what Mr. Mudd warned us about. One provocation could make the buttheads turn on us, and that's exactly what Quentin's picture did. Now it looked like they were going to destroy our planet, one city at a time. Talk about being oversensitive! I needed Lloyd more than ever. Only he could talk them out of it, but instead it was just me here, on my own. The fate of the planet rested on my shoulders. I was so terrified, I did something I had never done before.

I fear-farted.

Yes, I farted out of fear. I didn't even know it was possible, but apparently, my butt did.

IAmAWeenieBurger whipped his head around instantly. "Watch your mouth!" he admonished. I don't even know what I said, but I guess I fart-cursed.

Very nervously, I stepped into my bedroom and shut the door behind me so my parents wouldn't know that a plot to destroy our planet was being hatched there. "Please don't kill us all!" I whimpered.[14]

IAmAWeenieBurger put down his Sharpie, a hurt look on his face. "Hold on, bro. You think we're going to kill you?"

"That's why you're drawing X's on my planet, isn't it? Those are the places you're going to attack?"

Doodoofartmama rolled his eyes. "FRRT!" he laughed.

"You're not going to kill us?" I said. It was kind of cool that I knew what he meant, even without taking

---

14   If this is getting too intense for you, take a little break and read our blog on parents, on page 268—unless you are a parent, in which case, please don't read what we really think of you.

a sniff. I was actually starting to understand their language.

IAmAWeenieBurger rested one of his three hands on my shoulder. "Like I said, man, on our planet there's no war; everyone's just chill. So the thought of attacking never entered our buttheads. I forgot humans were such jerks."

"But if you're not going to attack, then why did you cross out Paris?"

"We didn't cross it out. We renamed it!" He pointed to the X on the globe. "That's what we'll be calling Paris now!"

"And Tokyo? And Seattle? You renamed them all X?"

"FRRT!" Doodoofartmama was laughing his head off.

"Those aren't X's!" IAmAWeenieBurger explained. "We're using our written language. If you look closely, you'll see the two lines meet at different angles each time. That's how we differentiate our words." He pointed to Paris. "Paris will now be called FRRT!" He tooted out a bouquet of perfume and strawberry crepes.

Then, he pointed to Chicago. "And Chicago will be called FRRT!" This fart smelled like deep-dish pizza.

The difference in the sound was subtle, but it was noticeable. Sure enough, when I looked, the two *X*'s weren't identical either. Paris was like this:

And Chicago was more like this:

"So you're not going to take over the Earth?"

"Of course not! Our homies are just coming to hang out! No biggie."

"Actually, it's kind of a biggie," I warned him. "Quentin already knows you're here, and soon other people will, too."

"Aw!" IAmAWeenieBurger mussed my hair with his fingerless hand. "You Earthlings are adorable when you're needlessly concerned."

"You mean you're not worried humans will hurt you? Um, haven't you seen what we do to aliens in movies?"

"Oh yes. And we have learned from the mistakes the fictional aliens have made. We're not just sending one or two thousand buttheads. We've invited seventy billion of our closest friends! We'll outnumber you ten to one."

"Seventy billion?" I gasped. "You're talking about an invasion!"

"I guess that's the closest Earth word for it," IAmAWeenieBurger said cheerfully. "Though grasshoppers are a little more precise when they call it a—" He rubbed his legs together, making a *chirp-chirp* sound. "Don't worry," IAmAWeenieBurger explained. "This will all be much simpler when we make FRRT the official language of Earth."

"You're going to change our language?"

"Well, yeah. It'll be much easier for us all when we talk the same, don't you think?"

"I guess," I said. "But why your language and not one of ours? Like Spanish?"

"Dude, it's so hard to trill those *r*'s," IAmAWeenie-Burger said. "And all that business with nouns being either male or female is kinda silly, don't you think? Everyone can fart, though. It's what bonds all the creatures of the universe." He was so calm and reassuring.

Maybe the aliens coming to our planet wouldn't be so bad after all. At least I wouldn't have to take Señora Acosta's class anymore. I could learn to speak in farts, I guess. I was already starting to understand Doodoofartmama.

"Is that all that's going to change?"

"Yes. Just that and a few minor little things. Like we'll be bringing Snertflings with us, of course."

"What are Snertflings?"

"They're our pets." He started talking in a cutesy voice, the way someone does to a puppy. "They're fluffy and cuddly and have big cute wittle eyes, and you just wanna squeeze 'em, you do!"

"They sound OK. And they'll get along with cats and dogs?"

"Well, Snertflings do get a bit territorial, to be honest."

"A bit?"

"They usually eat any other pets they come across. But we'll work on it."

I was starting to get nervous again. I decided to dig a bit deeper. "What about the government? Will we still be a democracy? Will people have the right to vote?"

"Of course! We wouldn't mess with your system of government. Democracy rocks, yo."

"OK, whew," I sighed.

"Then again, we'll outnumber you ten to one, so buttheads will probably control the Senate, the House, the Supreme Court, the White House, and most state legislatures. Don't worry, though. We'll amp up your quality of life by giving you new, less stressful jobs."

"New jobs? But what about important people like doctors or lawyers? Even teachers?

"Oh, silly you! We won't need humans to heal us, teach us, or mediate disputes. We're so much more intelligent than you single-brained life-forms. Besides, we've heard your parents talking. All they do is complain about their jobs. So we'll have Earthlings do things that are very low pressure. Wouldn't they like that?"

I tried to imagine my parents not complaining about work. They'd hardly be the same people anymore. "What kind of jobs are you talking about?"

"Well, we'll need skilled laborers to build landing pods for our spaceships and toilets you can rest your head on. The rest of your humans will be put on brain jam duty."

"Brain jam?"

"Yeah, it's, like, this sticky gunk that accumulates between our toes. We don't always have time to dig it out ourselves, so humans will pick it out for us and then dump it in a big giant tub of acid. Trust me, it's way cool if you can stand the smell."

"Um . . ." I wanted to protest, but I didn't know where to begin. Lloyd was the king of persuasion. The only thing I could think of to say was, "Oh, just blow us up already." Thankfully, before I could speak, Doodoofartmama interrupted with a massive sneeze.

"Uhh-SHOOZ!" Snot spurted out of his toes across my bedroom floor.

"Of course," IAmAWeenieBurger said, "we've gotta fix your planet's germ problem, man. I mean, it can't be too hard to find a cure for the common cold, right?"

"Please, no! Don't do this!"

"But they're already on their way. Doodoofartmama just invited them."

"When?" I asked. "When are they getting here?"

"They'll arrive here on FRRT in two days," IAmAWeenieBurger said. He paused, then added, "Oh yes, by the way, the new name of your planet is FRRT."

This fart smelled like McDonald's.

# CHAPTER 14

As I walked to school the next morning, I wondered how much longer Earth would continue to look like the planet I'd come to know. There would be new buildings soon—and new faces everywhere I went, many of them with butts on them. Some of my neighbors would have spaceships parked in their driveways and their yards would be full of Snertflings, whatever those were. I wondered what else would change.

Would aliens adopt our culture, or would we behave more like them? Would humans start giving their kids names like IAmAWeenieBurger? Would we have a President Doodoofartmama? Would buttheads star in all our TV shows and movies? Would the next Spider-Man be a Spider-Butthead?[15]

I wondered how long it would take me to learn their language, and if I'd have to drink more soda so I could fart out everything that was on my mind. I was pretty sure my parents would never quite get the hang of it, and they'd constantly be asking me to translate for them when a butthead song came on the radio or a breaking news report interrupted their favorite TV show, *The Big Bang Butt Factor*. That made me wonder if buttheads would keep our old songs in their native tongues, the way we do with operas, or if everything would be rerecorded with farts. Some songs might actually sound better that way.

Then I wondered if buttheads would bring their own religions with them, with butthead gods and a butthead bible? Or would they just tell us which one of our belief systems was the right one? "We appreciate your multi-millennia-spanning quest for spiritual enlightenment, but let's end the suspense. The true religion is Shintoism." Then suddenly, there'd be no more Christmas or Passover and we'd get off from school on Japanese New Year.

---

15  See page 270 for our blog about aliens, or at least what we thought we knew about them before we actually met any.

As soon as I saw Lloyd, I ran up to his locker to tell him the news. He would know what to do.

"Eh, we had a good run." Lloyd shrugged. He hung up his coat and his backpack and waited for me so we could walk to homeroom together.

"Lloyd, we can't just give up our planet to the buttheads!" I said. "This is the only planet we have. The only one we know how to get to!" I grabbed my US history textbook for first period and closed my locker. "Will you talk to them? You're a master at getting people to do what you want."

"Yeah, *people*," Lloyd said. "I don't know how to talk to these things. I'm not even sure where to look, to be honest. Their eyes? Their mouths? Their butts? And you said they outnumber us ten to one. How am I going to convince seventy billion aliens of anything?"

He was right, of course. This was an intergalactic takeover we were talking about, with humans versus far superior creatures from across the universe. What were the odds that two barely twelve-year-old kids like us could save all of humankind in a situation like this?

Then I saw Quentin heading to the principal's office to do the morning announcements. This was all his fault. He and his stupid picture ruined everything. I wanted to shout, "Traitor!" down the hall, but I realized that would only make me look like the crazy one.

"Hold on," I said to Lloyd. "What if you don't have to convince them? What if you just convince one annoying Earthling instead?" I waved for Lloyd to follow me, and I took off down the hall.

Lloyd and I caught up to Quentin. It was pretty clear what his "few measured words" would be about today, unless we could stop him.

"Quentin, you can't tell anyone about what you saw yesterday," Lloyd said.

"It's too late!" he replied. "I posted my picture all over social media, and my profile is skyrocketing. I've already been retweeted by The Area 51 Club, and the E.T. Truther Movement faved me! This guy @AlienzRSoReallyReal was messaging me all night for more information. So I called a press conference for tomorrow morning, and every news crew in town is coming."

"This has gone too far," I said. "Because of you, the aliens are planning to come and take over the Earth!"

Quentin snickered. "All the more reason I should tell everyone about them. I'm going to be the kid who saved the whole planet!"

"Only if we win," Lloyd said. "And if we lose, you'll be the first one picking out toe jam."

"Huh?" Quentin said.

"They're going to enslave us all. If you want to be the kid who saved Earth, help us convince them to leave." Lloyd was doing it. I could see him actually getting through to Quentin. "Forget those lists of kids who'll change the world someday. You'll be the kid who did change the world. The biggest hero in human history."

It was working. Quentin was deep in thought, nodding softly as he realized Lloyd was right.

"Oh, Mr. President!" Principal Hartley stuck her head out of her office. "We're ready for you." She waved him inside and handed him a sheet of paper. "Here are today's announcements, after your few measured words, of course. I can't wait to hear what you have to share with us today!"

Quentin followed her into the office. Lloyd and I waited outside to see what would happen. "Do you think he'll do it?" I asked.

"I don't know," Lloyd said. "We tried our best."

While we waited anxiously for Quentin's announcements to start, we saw someone waving to us from down the hall. "Guys! Guys! Did you see?" Kaitlyn

Wien-Tomita pushed her way through the crowd to reach us.

"You mean the Instagram post?" I asked.

"No, I mean my video report on the Smart-Off. It just passed a thousand views. My most ever!"

"That's fantastic!" Lloyd replied. Amid all our dread about Quentin's picture, we had forgotten about the Smart-Off.

Kaitlyn handed us her phone so we could see the video. "Look!" she said. "It's getting linked all over the place!" She showed us a page which had posted the video under the headline: "Hotheaded Dweeb Goes Mental After Losing Brainiac Competition." Underneath that was a still frame of Quentin standing on a cafeteria table after the Smart-Off tryouts, in the middle of a deranged scream.

Lloyd burst out laughing. "Oh, man! He looks psycho!"

It was exactly the revenge we had always wanted, but I couldn't celebrate, because at that moment, the speakers crackled with feedback, signaling the start of morning announcements.

"Attention, fellow students," Quentin began. His voice was shaky and uncertain. "This is your president,

Quentin Fairchild, speaking, and today, I'd like to say a few measured words about . . ." He took a deep breath. ". . . about aliens."

"Ooh!" Kaitlyn said, grabbing her phone back. "This story keeps getting better!" She held her phone and darted into Principal Hartley's office to capture the moment.

There was a long pause in the announcements right then. I could hear Principal Hartley whispering to Quentin in the background. "Quentin, are you all right? Quentin?"

Quentin continued, his voice quivering. "You've probably seen my Instagram picture from yesterday and heard about my press conference for tomorrow morning. Well, I'd like to say now that . . . that . . that it was all a hoax. There are no aliens."

Lloyd and I high-fived. I suddenly felt what it was like to save a planet. It felt pretty good.

"In other announcements . . ." Quentin continued sadly. I heard him rustle the paper Principal Hartley had given him, and he began to read. "The Smart-Off tryouts were yesterday. Congratulations to everyone who made the team, especially . . ."

Another long pause. His voice started to warp with

anger. "Especially the new Super Brain . . ." I heard him grumbling, and then he tore the paper into pieces. "No!" he shouted. "I can't lie anymore! There *are* aliens! And they're helping students cheat on the Smart-Off competition! I'm the real Super Brain! Me!"

"Quentin, what are you—?" We could hear Principal Hartley scrambling behind him.

"Aliens are coming to take over the Earth, and their first step was dethroning me as the Super Brain! We need to mobilize! Join me in the fight! Put down your textbooks and pick up your ray guns! THIS IS OUR PLANET, AND WE NEED TO DEFEND IT!"

He sounded pretty insane at this point, screaming so loudly that every syllable he spat into the microphone was accompanied by horrible feedback.

Then, suddenly, everything got quiet again. "I'm terribly sorry about that outburst," Principal Hartley said. "Have a nice day. Oh, and please note that the chess team will meet in Room 233 today, as their usual room is being repainted. Thank you."

A weird hush fell over the hallway. All I could hear were the sound of footsteps—urgent, pounding against the linoleum, getting closer and closer. Quentin emerged from the principal's office, tailed by Kaitlyn and her camera. He was absolutely seething at me and Lloyd. Then, a man rounded the corner. We saw his hair before we saw him, then his rainbow-striped pants and suspenders.

"What do you know?" he shouted. Lloyd, Quentin, and me all looked at Mr. Mudd, as he grabbed Quentin by the shoulders and got right in his face. "Do they like video games? Do they fart conversationally? Where are their butts?" He shook Quentin, demanding an answer. "Where. Are. Their. Butts?"

Lloyd and I shared a concerned look, but Quentin just thought Mr. Mudd had finally gone off the deep end.

"What are you talking about?" Quentin asked.

"I saw your picture on Instagram. I tried to message you all night!"

"You're @AlienzRSoReallyReal?"

The bell rang and students filled the halls, heading to their first period classes. No one seemed worried about an alien takeover, which was a big relief. A few of them were snickering about Quentin's weird rant, but at least no one was freaking out.

"You fool!" Mr. Mudd shouted. "You've provoked them!"

"You're just going to have to come to my press conference!" Quentin snapped. "You, too, Kaitlyn," he said, turning toward Kaitlyn's phone. "If I decide to give you media credentials, that is." He stuck his hand in Kaitlyn's lens, and she turned the camera off.

"That's fine," she said, putting her camera away. "I've got plenty for a new post! Thanks!" She skipped off down the hallway, happily, which only made Quentin angrier.

More than anything at that moment, I wanted to talk to Mr. Mudd. Clearly, he had more information on the aliens than Lloyd and I previously thought. We would've asked him for a private chat, if Principal Hartley hadn't come out of her office looking for us. "Come on in, boys. All three of you. Let's talk."

She waved us in, and we shrugged at Mr. Mudd. We were curious to know what information he had, but that conversation would have to wait.

✪

Quentin showed Principal Hartley the picture he'd taken on his cell phone. "They're in his house!" Quentin said, pointing his finger at me. He zoomed in on the image. "And if you look closely, you'll see a butt crack on the back of his head!"

Principal Hartley took the phone from Quentin for a closer look. "I've never seen anything like this before," she said. She actually seemed like she believed Quentin. Thankfully, Lloyd was ready.

"I don't believe in aliens myself, Principal Hartley," Lloyd lied. "And I think Josh would've noticed if there were creatures from another planet in his house. Right, Josh?"

Principal Hartley put on her glasses and zoomed in on the alien in the picture. "It does look like a butt crack," she nodded.

"Well, it's very easy to fake a picture these days, as you know," Lloyd said. "It's not as easy to fool a woman as smart as you."

"Hmmm . . ." Principal Hartley nodded. She took off her glasses and handed back the phone. "Quentin, are you sure you're not just upset about losing the captain slot on the Smart-Off team?"

Quentin leapt out of his seat, pointing his finger at me and shouting at the top of his voice. "He cheated!" he yelled. "I'm smarter than Josh! I should be the captain!"

"Mmm-hmm," Principal Hartley nodded. "That's what I figured."

Things were going pretty well for me and Lloyd. Quentin was sounding like a certified lunatic. Principal Hartley shook her head, disappointed in him. "Quentin, I guess you had your moment as our local star. Now it looks like it's time to give the spotlight to someone else."

"Uh . . . uh . . ." Quentin wanted to argue, but he couldn't get any sound to come out. He looked like he might cry. I actually felt a little bad for him. I'd dreamed about this ever since Quentin made his first magazine cover and started treating me and Lloyd like inferiors. We'd beaten him. We'd taken down a giant.

Technically, of course, everything he was saying was true.

"Now, boys, please go to class." Principal Hartley shooed us out of her office. From behind her closed door, we could hear her moan to herself, "I can't wait for Spring Break!"

✺

After school, I wanted to rush right home and try to save the Earth, but Lloyd insisted we go to Smart-Off practice instead. "You've earned this, Josh," he told me. "Don't you deserve one moment on top before the planet is taken over by buttheads?" He had a point.

As soon as I walked in, all the other Smarties stood up and applauded for me. Except Quentin, of course. He sat perfectly still, with his arms folded across his chest and a bitter scowl on his face. He'd been demoted to Science Smarty.

It was fun being the leader of something for a change. I got to pick the color for our team uniforms: tie-dye. I got to choose our official team snack: Chocolatey-Flavored Gummy Grahams. And when I suggested the team name "The Number Twos," everyone voted for it except guess who. (I thought it'd be so cool when we won and the announcer had to say, "This week's number one is . . . The Number Twos!") But the best part was watching Quentin grit his teeth and pout the whole time. I tried not to stare. After all, Kaitlyn was filming it, so I knew I'd be able to grab some sweet screencaps of his frowny face later on.

It was all going great until we reached the part where we actually started practicing, and I had to answer some questions. I was hoping the method that worked so well for me during the tryouts would pay off again, but it turns out yelling the first thing that comes into your head is only a good strategy when an alien eyeball is beaming you the answers.

"Eighteen?" the Language Arts Smarty asked. "You sure that's your answer?"

"Yeah, sure," I said.

"No, sorry," she replied. "The correct answer is photosynthesis."

Each time it happened, Quentin got angrier and angrier, until finally, when I replied that the capital of China was Kung Pao Town. That was apparently the final straw.

"AUUUUUGGGHHHH!" he shouted. He leapt out of his seat and gave me a huge shove that knocked me to the ground. "You JERK!" Then he dove to the floor and started attacking. It was a rapid volley of slaps and elbows, each one punctuated by a wimpy squeal. "I! Hate! You! Ehhh!"

The other Smarties formed a circle around us to watch the melee. The Language Arts Smarty wondered if she should get a faculty member, while the Math Smarty kept pumping his fist and saying, "Fight! Fight! Fight!" Kaitlyn was there, too, filming every limp punch Quentin threw. (She was the Tech Smarty.)

All of them realized pretty quickly, though, that Quentin wasn't actually hitting me. He was hitting my backpack, but he had his eyes closed, like it was too painful for him to watch his own meltdown, so he didn't realize that I was quietly sitting next to him, watching.

"Josh, you OK?" Lloyd asked.

I shrugged and slid backward across the floor, as Quentin started kicking, blindly beating the crap out of my backpack.

"You! Deserve! This!"

"This is lame," the Math Smarty said, and he walked away, bored. Others followed his lead, and the Smarties sat back down and peppered each other with trivia questions. Everyone seemed to know the fight was over, except Quentin, who was still kicking and swinging his arms at nothing in particular.

Again, I felt sorry for him. He couldn't even put on a fight that other kids were willing to watch. "Quentin, stop," I said.

"Never!" he yelled. "I don't care if I get expelled! It'll be worth it!"

"Dude," Lloyd said, yanking my backpack out of Quentin's teeth. (I think he thought he was biting my arm or something.) "You're squishing Josh's homework."

Finally, Quentin opened his eyes. He looked around, as if snapping out of a trance. "I guess you've had enough," he said, and he stood up to brush himself off.

"Look, I don't want to fight," I told him. Lloyd and I pulled him aside, where no one else could hear us. "Not with you or the aliens. Can't you just help us get rid of them?"

"You mean, I can meet them?" Quentin said. He calmed down and stared at me hopefully.

"Sure you can!" Lloyd jumped in. "Are you kidding? They're dying to meet you!" He looked at me and winked. We should've guessed sooner that playing to Quentin's ego was the way to go.

"Really?" Quentin said.

"Yeah," Lloyd continued. "They have statues of you all over their planet. Your picture is, like, on their money."

"You're making that up," Quentin said. "How do they know what I look like?"

"You're on the cover of all our magazines!" Lloyd said. "They think you're our leader."

Quentin smiled proudly, but he didn't seem totally convinced. "I'll believe it when I see it!"

"Then come see it!" Lloyd said. "Come to Josh's house and meet them!"

"What?" I said. "He can't come to my house!"

"That's right, I can't," Quentin replied defiantly. "I'm not going to come to your house so you can play another trick on me and humiliate me more. I'll meet the aliens, and I'll consider taking down my photo, but only if they come to my house."

"That's impossible!" I said. "How are we supposed to get them to your house without anyone seeing them?"

"We'll do it," Lloyd interrupted. "One hour from now, your place. Be ready."

Quentin smiled and reached out his hand. "Gentlemen, you have a deal."

We shook his hand. Then, he spun around and started marching away. He got only two steps before stumbling over his own backpack and nearly faceplanting on the floor. "Ow! I'm all right! I'm all right!" He regained his balance, picked up his bag, and left.

"I don't know, Lloyd," I said. "We're putting an awful lot of faith in Quentin to save the world."

"I'm not putting any faith in him," Lloyd replied. "We're going to take this to a higher authority."

"The FBI?"

Lloyd shook his head. "Not quite."

# CHAPTER 15

Mr. Mudd had his face pressed against his computer screen when we walked into class. There was a very blurry line running down the center, and that's about it, but he was examining it like a dog checks out a turd, with his face shoved in it, gazing from every possible angle. He kept pausing to take notes, as if each new glance gave him some deep insight.

"What's he looking at?" I asked Lloyd.

Lloyd shrugged.

"Amazing!" Mr. Mudd whispered to himself, as he jotted down another note.

On the whiteboard, he had already written up an assignment for tomorrow.

## ESSAY

An alien attack is imminent.

How will you plead for mercy?

What is your plan to save the human race from utter annihilation?

(500 words or less)

As we were contemplating his essay question, he finally saw us standing in the room, and he waved us over.

"You really think we humans can save ourselves by pleading for mercy?" I asked him.

Mr. Mudd had a hearty laugh. "Oh no! Not anyone in my class, at least. It's just busywork. Have a seat, boys." He pointed to two chairs set up across from his desk. "I trust you know what this is." He glanced back at his computer screen.

"The Grand Canyon?" I asked.

"A blurry line?" Lloyd guessed.

"It's from Quentin's picture." Mr. Mudd clicked on a few buttons, and the picture zoomed out wide. Sure enough, once it did, we could see that what he had been looking at was the back of IAmAWeenieBurger's head.

"Dude, that's an alien butt!" Lloyd said.

"Of course! I should've known!" Mr. Mudd said, slapping his forehead. "Had he been eating Oreos?"

Lloyd and I shared an impressed look. "How did you know that?" I asked.

"I think it's time for you boys to tell me everything you know."

"Well, I know two plus two is four, and *i* before *e* except after *c*," Lloyd said. "Now what do you know?"

"I know more than you think I do," Mr. Mudd said, ominously.

I looked at Lloyd, and he nodded. I'd been longing for this moment, a chance to tell the story to someone who'd actually believe it and to get their advice. To warn them about the invasion and see if they had any last-ditch ideas to save humanity. To no longer have to carry this burden entirely on our own. I took a deep breath and thought hard about how to begin.

"They have butts on their heads!" I shouted.

After that, Lloyd took over. He told Mr. Mudd the whole story. How the aliens showed up at Chop Socky, how they played my video games, and how seventy billion more of them were on their way here right now. I kept waiting for Mr. Mudd to fall off his chair or spit out his drink in shock and horror, but he didn't seem surprised at all. He just nodded along, as if it was exactly what he expected to hear.

"And you didn't say anything," Mr. Mudd said, "because you wanted to protect them. Because you believed they came in peace. And because no one would believe twelve-year-old boys talking about aliens with butts on their heads, who spoke in farts. Is that right?"

"Whoa!" I replied. "How do you know so much?"

"I know because those are the same reasons I kept quiet . . . when the aliens visited me!"

"What?"

Now it was Mr. Mudd's turn to tell his story. "I was your age," he said, "when they flew in my window one night. Two of them. IAmAWeenieBurger and Doodoofartmama."

"Those are our aliens!" Lloyd said.

"I figured. They said they needed somewhere to stay while they scoped out the Earth and figured out if it'd be worth invading. I'd just gotten my first Atari 2600 home video game system, so I distracted them by teaching them to play *Pac-Man*. I was hoping they'd lose interest in destroying our planet, but it only made them want to take it over even more. When they caught me taking a Polaroid picture of them, they flipped out and called their friends from home. Just that one small provocation was enough to make them want to invade. I begged them to spare us. I burned my picture in hopes they would just leave, and finally, they did. But as they left, they vowed to return in seven butthead years. I never got to ask them how long that was in Earth years, so I've dedicated my life since then to studying them and preparing for their invasion, knowing it could come any day."

"Well, it's coming tomorrow," Lloyd said. "So what do we do?"

"Don't worry, boys," Mr. Mudd replied confidently. "This is the moment I've been waiting for. And planning for. By day, I'm an ordinary teacher."

Lloyd and I shared a look. Mr. Mudd was anything but ordinary.

"By night, I am a pro-Earth crusader, scouring the Internet for information and planning for their arrival! Over the course of my life, I've developed and committed to memory a speech so persuasive that once the buttheads hear it, they will never return to our planet. All I need is a chance to deliver it before they take over."

"Well, we're taking them to Quentin's house after school."

"Quentin?" Mr. Mudd said. "Not him! He'll mess everything up!"

My jaw dropped. "You don't like him either?"

"Teachers can't stand weenies like him," Mr. Mudd explained. "Nobody can!"

I loved hearing that Mr. Mudd was no fan of Quentin's either, but unfortunately, I couldn't see any way of getting out of our meeting with him.

"Well, he'll really mess everything up if we don't let him meet the buttheads," I said.

"Why don't you come to his house with us?" Lloyd asked. "You can give your speech and make sure Quentin doesn't embarrass all of humankind."

"Boys, out of duty to our planet, I'll do it!"

I looked at Lloyd and smiled, starting to feel hopeful again that we could save Earth.

✪

As we walked back to my house after school, Lloyd did the math and figured out that we had three hours and twenty-two minutes before my parents got home from work. "That's plenty of time to take the buttheads to Quentin's!" he cheered. "We could even see a movie on the way home and still make it back in time!"

"Right," I said, "except that it's actually one hour and thirty-nine minutes before they get home."

"Oh."

Math was Lloyd's worst subject.

"So we'll just have to save the world a little bit faster," he said. He took off his digital watch. "I'll tell you what. It takes ten minutes to walk to Quentin's house. So that means we have to leave to come back here in one hour and twenty-three minutes."

"One hour and twenty-nine minutes," I corrected.

"Yes." He set his watch to count down from 01:29:00 and hit START. "Now we'll know how long we have."

Given that we had almost an hour and a half, I figured we could probably do it, but it wouldn't be easy. First, we had to explain to the buttheads why we wanted them to go.

Lloyd came up with a great lie to get them to Quentin's house. "Quentin's going to make a big announcement at a press conference," he said. "He'll let everyone know that your planet-mates are coming, so they don't get all freaked out when the sky fills up with UFOs and try to shoot them down."

"But I thought Quentin was a donkey-butt jerk," IAmAWeenieBurger said.

"He is," Lloyd said. "But he's a donkey-butt jerk people listen to."

They farted it over privately for a minute and then agreed it would be good to have someone spread their message.

Next, we needed to find a container we could use to transport the aliens. We had to search my whole house before we came across my parents' old cooler in the basement. We got the buttheads to go number four, but even still, we weren't sure we'd be able to get the lid closed.

"Ow! Ow! Ow!" IAmAWeenieBurger protested as Lloyd and I shoved him down on top of Doodoofartmama so we could get the latch to lock into place. With a final push, we got the cooler lid closed, and Lloyd and I bumped fists, confident about how our plan was proceeding.

"Let's go," he said, but when I got a look at the time on Lloyd's watch, I stopped short.

"An hour and four minutes," I said. I shook my head. "I can't go. We'll never make it in time."

"You have to come!" Lloyd said.

"Why? You can do it without me."

"No, I can't."

I couldn't believe how upset Lloyd was. "Sure you can," I told him. "I never really help with these plans anyway. We both know you get all the ideas and you do all the talking. I'm not important."

"Not important? Josh dude, you're essential." Lloyd grabbed me by the shoulders. I'd never seen him speak with such conviction before. This wasn't just a smooth-talking act like he sometimes pulled with grown-ups. This was for real. "You're the one who tried out for the Smart-Off, who pushed a stroller full of aliens across a parking lot, who let two creatures with butts on their heads sleep in his bedroom. You know why you did it and not me? Because I don't have the guts. I wouldn't even have the guts to talk to grown-ups if I didn't have you with me. You're my best friend, man. We're a team."

There were times when I wondered why I let Lloyd talk me into doing so many crazy things. Sometimes I even wondered why I was friends with him at all. But at that moment, I knew exactly why. At that moment, I would've done anything for him.

"OK," I smiled. "Let's go. But when that watch alarm goes off, we come back here, no matter what."

Lloyd nodded. "OK," he said. "Now come on. Let's go save the world."

Lloyd and I underestimated how heavy the cooler would be. Even with one of us on each side, we had to stop and take a break about every five seconds all the way to Quentin's house. By the time we got there, there were only forty-nine minutes left until my parents got home. I was already nervous about how fast time was ticking away. We rang the doorbell and waited. I was getting really impatient. "It's been eighteen seconds! What's taking him so long? If aliens were at my house, I'd answer the door in four or five seconds, tops."

The door swung open, and Quentin scowled at us. "Where are they?" he demanded, craning his neck to see behind us.

"In here," Lloyd said, pointing to the cooler.

Quentin looked at the cooler, skeptical. "I knew this was another trick!" He tried to slam the door on us, but Lloyd shoved the cooler inside to keep the door propped open.

"Guys, come on out," Lloyd said, flipping open the lid.

Quentin eased up on the door, staring at the cooler. "How dumb do you think I—" Before he could say "am," the two aliens rose up from the goo and took shape before Quentin's eyes. His jaw dropped, and he stood still, speechless, until finally Doodoofartmama broke the silence.

"FRRT!" he said, smiling and extending his hand.

The next sound I heard was a thud, as Quentin collapsed onto the floor, eyes closed.

"I think he fainted," Lloyd said. Lloyd and I bent down over Quentin to see if he was OK.

"Uhh-SHOOZ!"

"Bless you, Doodoofartmama," I said, looking over my shoulder.

Doodoofartmama shrugged, confused. "FRRT?"

I looked back at him, and to my shock, there was no snot at his feet. Instead, there was a sick puddle pooled up at IAmAWeenieBurger's feet. He was the one who sneezed this time.

"What just happened?" IAmAWeenieBurger said, confused.

"Uh-oh," I replied.

"Am I sick, too?" IAmAWeenieBurger whimpered.

"Uhh-SHOOZ!" He let out a second, bigger sneeze, and this time, the snot sprayed all over Quentin's face as he lay passed out on the floor.

"Maybe you guys shouldn't have done your business in the same container," I said. "All your germs must've mixed together."

"Germs are nasty little things!" IAmAWeenieBurger complained.

On the bright side, the blast of alien snot snapped Quentin back to consciousness. He began sputtering and rolled over. "What happened?"

"I snotted on you," IAmAWeenieBurger confessed. "Sorry, dude."

Quentin wiped the snot off his face and staggered to his feet, backing away in shock. "You're real!" he said. "I don't believe it. I have so many questions. Do you breathe oxygen? Can subatomic particles escape a black hole? Did *Star Trek* really happen?"

"Well, sit down," IAmAWeenieBurger said. "We have a lot to talk about, yo."

"Um, Lloyd . . ." I said. I pointed at the watch, as our time ticked quickly away.

"Right," Lloyd said. "Just take us to your room, Quentin. You'll have plenty of opportunities to dork out on these guys after they take over tomorrow."

"Hold on," Quentin said, leaning down over the cooler. He took a very close look at the gunk that was left behind after the buttheads took shape. "What is this?"

"Just some molten remnants from one of our many excretory processes." IAmAWeenieBurger shrugged. "No biggie."

Quentin reached into his pocket and whipped out a plastic baggie, then used it to scoop up some of the goo. "Fascinating," he said. He held it up to the light for a better look, then pressed it to his nose and took a good, long sniff.

As he backed away with his specimen, I pushed the cooler onto the front porch. Before I even closed the door, squirrels began to appear in the yard, sniffing their way toward it. I knew that by the time we were ready to go back, they would've licked it clean.

❂

I had never been to Quentin's basement laboratory before. It was dimly lit, and everywhere you looked, there were beakers bubbling with green and blue gunk, storage freezers marked "active culture" and "control culture," and vials hooked up to machines that were beeping constantly. On the wall were detailed diagrams of the anatomy of a cat and a pig.

"Pardon the mess," he said. "I've been working on a vaccine for feline swine flu."

We heard a creak, and a bright sliver of light spread down the stairway. "Hello!" Quentin's mom called from above. "There's a strange middle-aged man here to see you!" She led Mr. Mudd downstairs, with a tray of snacks in her hands. "And I have some goodies!"

I panicked, shoving the aliens toward a closet. "Guys! Hide!" I said. It was too late, though. She had already seen them—and they had seen Mr. Mudd.

"FRRT, Earl!" IAmAWeenieBurger said.

Mr. Mudd squeezed his face tight to respond in their language. "FRRT!" he replied, nodding to each of the buttheads as he popped off a nasty dook wave. "IAmAWeenieBurger, Doodoofartmama."

Doodoofartmama giggled.

"What's he laughing at?" Mr. Mudd asked.

"You fart with a funny accent," IAmAWeenieBurger admitted. "Nice try, though."

"Well, I see we all know each other here," Mrs. Fairchild said. "No need for introductions, eh?" She set her snack tray down, but nobody took anything. I didn't recognize a single item. All of the food was strangely colored and textured. None of what she was serving looked edible, let alone the kind of food you'd call "goodies." If I'd seen these objects in another context, I might've guessed they were car parts or structures used for shelter by small sea creatures. I would never have guessed any of these supposed foods she was serving us were even fit for human consumption.

Lloyd was far less tactful than me. "What is that stuff?" he asked.

Quentin's mom smiled and pointed to the items on the plate. "These are dried kiwi flakes. Coconut leather. Dairy-free flaxseed brownies. A few cups of rose petal tea to wash it down. And for a little guilty pleasure, I threw in some carob chips."

Even with everything I'd been through the last few days, this was the most disgusting thing I'd ever seen.

"What about Oreos?" IAmAWeenieBurger asked.

Quentin's mom giggled, "Well, we eat healthy around here!" she said. "But I'll see what I can whip up."

"Thank you!" IAmAWeenieBurger called out, as she bobbed back up the stairs. "Nice lady."

I felt a little bad that we had insulted her food, but then I realized I could use it to our advantage. "Guys," I said, "Earth isn't all video games and Oreos, you know. There's lots of food like this, too."

"Hey, I love coconut leather!" Quentin said, stuffing his face.

As the aliens sniffed the snack platter with their feet, I leaned in to whisper to Quentin. "Remember, we're trying to get them not to take over the Earth, right?"

Quentin nodded. "Right."

"How have you been, Muddy?" IAmAWeenieBurger said. "Still trying to beat our high score on *Space Invaders*?" He laughed mockingly.

"That third hand is an unfair advantage on shooters!" Mr. Mudd retorted, clearly stung by the jab.

"Whoa, calm down," Lloyd said, pulling him aside. "Remember, we need to get them to call off their invasion, even if we have to kiss their buttheads."

"Right," Mr. Mudd agreed. "Then I should give my speech!"

"Not yet," Lloyd replied. "First, Quentin should tell them he's taking down the picture and saying it was a hoax. Then, they won't feel threatened by Earthlings anymore."

"Aha. Good idea," Mr. Mudd agreed.

"Buttheads," Lloyd said to the aliens. "Quentin has something he wants to talk to you about." He winked at me, and we both winked at Mr. Mudd. This was going perfectly according to plan.

"Sure," Quentin said. "But first, can I see your money?"

"What?" Lloyd said, caught off guard.

"You want to see woofbas?" IAmAWeenieBurger asked. "But Josh says they are worthless on your planet."

"I just want to see the picture," Quentin said, grinning.

I turned to Lloyd, panicked. I had totally forgotten that Lloyd told Quentin he was on their money. Clearly, though, it had been on Quentin's mind.

IAmAWeenieBurger reached inside his butt. "Well, I wouldn't have guessed you were such a fan of Queen Turdmuncher, but here you go." He pulled out a piece of money, much like our own but with a drawing of a butt where one of our presidents would be.

"Queen who?" Quentin said, looking at the bill. "That's not me!"

"No, that's how they pictured you," Lloyd insisted. "And Queen Turdmuncher is your name on their planet. It's a pretty good name for you." Even he could tell at this point he wasn't being very convincing.

"You lied!" Quentin said. "I'm not on their money! They probably don't even have more than three or four statues of me on their entire planet!"

IAmAWeenieBurger laughed. "Just the one, actually. The Snertflings love to pee on it."

"What?" Quentin shouted. "Is this a joke?"

"Quentin, let me explain," Lloyd said.

Quentin cut him off. He was furious. "I want to talk to the aliens," he demanded. "Without you guys!"

He opened the door to the basement bathroom. "Ooh, you're busted," IAmAWeenieBurger said to me as the aliens filed in.

"Mr. Mudd, you have to go with them," I said. "Make sure Quentin gets them to agree not to invade."

"Of course," Mr. Mudd replied. "Don't worry, boys. I've been preparing for this my whole life!"

Mr. Mudd followed Quentin and the buttheads into the bathroom and closed the door behind them, leaving Lloyd and me alone in his lab. "Do you think this'll work?" Lloyd asked.

"It has to," I said. "Those two don't want to pick toe jam any more than we do."

At the top of the stairs, the door opened, and

Quentin's mom returned with a new tray of snacks. "Hi-ho, boys!" she said. "I made some organic Oreos!"

She showed us what she'd made, but they looked nothing like Oreos. They were square and green, and the middle was much wetter and mushier.

"Well, you'll have to give me the recipe," Lloyd said, trying to be polite.

"It's easy!" she said. "It's just raw tofu between two strips of dehydrated seaweed. Try it!"

"I wish I could," Lloyd said. "But I'm seaweed intolerant."

"Well, just give it to the buttheads when they come out."

It was a little strange how friendly she was to the two freakish monsters her son brought into her basement, and once she called them buttheads, I knew something was up.

"How come you're not weirded out by the aliens?" I asked.

"Well, I read every single post on the *Peaceful Extraterrestrial's Guide to Earth* blog. I was wondering when I'd run into those fellas."

"So you were one of the other likes on all our blog posts!" I said.

"Of course," she boasted. "I'm very proud of my netiquette."

"I still wonder who that fourth like was from," I said.

"Nobody I know." Mrs. Fairchild shrugged. "I didn't even tell Quenty about the blog, not since you badmouthed him so much."

"Um, sorry about that," I said.

"Oh, I was a kid once, too. I love my Quenty, but I can see why you might sometimes call him a . . . what was the term, a horse butt creep?" She looked fondly toward the bathroom. "What are they doing in there anyway?"

I sighed. "Just determining the fate of the planet."

"Fun!" she replied, and then she scurried back upstairs.

# CHAPTER 16

Lloyd and I listened at the bathroom door. We were hoping we'd hear the sounds of a historic peace accord being brokered, or at least get a heads-up if our planet was doomed.

"All I hear is lots of farting," I said.

"Sorry, that was me," Lloyd confessed. "Those flax-seed brownies were surprisingly tasty."

It was no use. We backed away from the door and started walking around the room. "I just hope they hurry," I said. "How long do we have?"

I could tell from the look on Lloyd's face that it wasn't long. "Um, six minutes till we have to leave."

I groaned, gazing around the room to take my mind off the time. I realized Quentin was working on a lot more projects than I ever would've guessed. Vaccines, medicines, inventions. There must've been a hundred ways he was working to make the world a little bit better.

"You see that?" Lloyd said.

"Yeah, maybe he's not so bad," I admitted.

"What? I'm talking about his shrine to himself." He pointed to a display case full of awards, plaques, and framed magazine covers, all proclaiming how special Quentin was. There was a trophy in the shape of a cat and another one in the shape of a syringe. There was his *Newsweek* cover, along with one for *Scientific American* and a *Rolling Stone* where he listed his favorite songs about medicine and/or cats. Lloyd was pretending like he was about to throw up, but I couldn't help feeling like Quentin had earned everything in there. He worked hard for his accomplishments. Why shouldn't he be proud?

"What if we're the donkey-butt jerks, Lloyd?" I said.

"Us! Why would you say that?"

"Because we've spent all this time trying to make him look bad. Trying to outdo him. And why? He's done a lot of good things." I picked up a vial labeled Feline Chicken Pox Vaccine. "Look, he cured a disease. Maybe he's allowed to have a bit of an ego."

Lloyd took the vial from me. He clearly hadn't heard

a word I said. "I wonder if we can use this to bargain. Tell the aliens if they go home, they can have it. Then, they'll never get feline chicken pox on their planet."

"That's a terrible idea," I replied. "A vaccine is just a weakened version of a virus. Our bodies are used to viruses, so a small dose helps us learn how to defend against it. The aliens have never known diseases like ours, so they don't have the same immune systems. This little bit of virus could make them very sick."

"I guess," Lloyd said. "They're so whiny about having a little cold, I can only imagine how they'd handle chicken pox."

"Maybe we need to grow up," I sighed. I gazed at the bathroom door. "Any second now, he'll come bursting out of there telling us he saved the world."

Before Lloyd could respond, the bathroom door flew open. Quentin spread his arms out and proclaimed, "I've saved the world!"

I smiled at Lloyd, relieved. I couldn't believe it, but I actually wanted to hug Quentin.

"You worked everything out?" Lloyd asked.

"Absolutely!" IAmAWeenieBurger said. "Quentin made some awesome points. And Muddy's speech was killer."

"Aw, thanks," Mr. Mudd blushed.

Lloyd shook his head. "Well, buttheads, I'll be sad to see you go."

"Go?" IAmAWeenieBurger said. "No. We're not going."

"Mr. Mudd," I said, "didn't you convince them that they have to leave?"

Mr. Mudd shuffled his feet. "Well, they found my speech quite persuasive, but then they had a speech of their own, and wow, that really changed everything."

"A speech of their own?" I repeated, nervously.

"Yes!" IAmAWeenieBurger said. "We declared that we will never leave the great planet of Quentonia."

"What?"

IAmAWeenieBurger shrugged. "Mr. Mudd explained how seventy billion buttheads showing up was gonna be a little weird for you guys. So we agreed to make a few changes to smooth things over. Let your new leader tell you about it." He motioned toward Quentin.

"Our new leader?" I said.

"Well, officially my title will be the Ultimate Supreme President of the Native Residents of Quentonia."

"Does this mean we won't be stuck picking junk out of their toes?" I asked.

"Well, *we* won't," Quentin said, motioning to

himself and Mr. Mudd. "I'll be too busy overseeing the design of our new currency, Quentmarks." He held up a roughly sketched dollar bill, with a drawing of his smiling face right in the center.

"That's what you were doing in there?" I shouted, ripping the drawing from his hands. "That's what you were negotiating?"

"You sold us out!" Lloyd said. "And Mr. Mudd! You should be ashamed. What did they make you? Super President?"

IAmAWeenieBurger bowed his head. "He will be the Assistant Undersecretary of Submission and Subservience."

"That's what you sold us out for?"

"It's a growth position," Mr. Mudd said with a shrug.

Lloyd stood up on a chair, fuming. "Enough! We need to start this negotiation over, right now, and we won't stop until—"

*BEEP! BEEP! BEEP!*

"Lloyd," I interrupted. I nodded toward his watch as its alarm sounded.

"Josh, the fate of the world . . ." Lloyd said.

"Yeah, but my parents," I reminded him. "You promised."

Lloyd nodded and shut off the stopwatch. He quietly stepped down from the chair. "Never mind." He sighed. "Josh and I have to go."[16]

✪

We walked back to my house, dragging the cooler behind us in silence. Doodoofartmama wanted to stay at Quentin's, but IAmAWeenieBurger thought it would be easier for the seventy billion aliens on their way to Earth to find them if they stayed at my place. Plus, Quentin didn't have any video games, and IAmAWeenieBurger was hoping to start playing *Galacto Blast 8* before the invasion began.

I wanted to kick myself for ever thinking Quentin was a good guy. He only cared about himself. If anything, we'd been too nice to him. If only the whole world knew the real Quentin. Now I'd be home just in time to face my parents, only to have to break the news to them that I'd handed the Earth over to a bunch of buttheads, including the biggest butthead of all, Quentin Fairchild.

"We should take this cooler and leave it on the freeway," Lloyd said. "Maybe a truck will run over it."

---

16 Sometimes, allowing aliens to destroy the Earth is just the kind of thing you do for your friends. Read more about friends in our blog on page 272.

"Someone could get hurt, though," I said.

"Then we should bury it in toxic waste at the bottom of a landfill!"

I shook my head. "That might just turn them into mighty mutated super-aliens."

Lloyd nodded in agreement. We both knew we were too peaceful and nice to do the buttheads any real harm.

Then suddenly, Lloyd stopped walking. "Hey, Josh. What's that thing?"

We looked ahead of us on the sidewalk, where a furry creature with a big bushy tail stared at us with angry eyes. As we looked back at it, it hissed and then scurried away, racing up a tree trunk in a split second. I barely got a look at it, but it was like nothing I'd ever seen.

"I don't know, but it seemed diseased," I said. "Maybe President Quentin can cure it when he's done putting his face on Mount Rushmore."

"Uh-oh," Lloyd said. "That reminds me." He reached into his pocket and pulled out the vial of Feline Chicken Pox vaccine.

"You took that with you?" I asked.

"I was mad. I wanted to do something mean. I guess I'll just throw it away before it gets the aliens sick."

He went to toss it in the bushes, but I grabbed his arm. "Wait. That's actually not a bad idea."

"What do you mean?"

I opened the cooler, where our two mushed-up friends sloshed around in one big brick of burnt sienna slush.

"Josh, what are you doing?" Lloyd asked. The butthead eyes sloshed around in the foul pool of number four, and as Lloyd spoke, they turned and peered upward at him.

I quickly pulled him aside and whispered softly to him. "Lloyd, they're just going to the bathroom in there. Remember, they can still hear us."

He nodded and lowered his voice. "You said it would be bad to give them the vaccine!" [17]

"Only if we want them to stay healthy. Maybe a little feline chicken pox will finally change their feelings about this planet."

"Whoa, that's harsh, Josh!" Lloyd said. I think he was actually kind of impressed with me.

"Those buttheads messed with the wrong planet," I replied. "See if you can distract them while I pour it in."

---

17 This will probably make more sense after you've read our blog on vaccines, on page 273. (Or possibly not. It's a complicated topic.)

"On it," Lloyd said, confidently. I followed him back over to the cooler, sure he was devising another genius plan. "Hey, look! Oreos!" he shouted, pointing off into the distance.

The four butthead eyes all followed him, and I knew I only had a second to make this work. I ripped off the top of the vial and poured the vaccine into the swirling butthead soup. Success. I managed to sneak it in without them seeing.

"Oh, never mind," Lloyd said to the disappointed aliens. "It was just a Chips Ahoy."

We closed the lid to the cooler and continued our sad march home. All I could do now was cross my fingers on the remote chance that this crazy plan might actually work.

# CHAPTER 17

My parents were due to get home so soon that Lloyd and I lugged that cooler in record time. When we finally shoved it through my front door, we were so exhausted we both wanted to collapse. We couldn't, though; not yet. We still had to carry the cooler upstairs to my room. We took it one agonizing step at a time. *Thump! Thump! Thump!* It felt like it would be hours before we'd reach the top of the staircase.

We had about three steps left to go when I heard my parents' car pull up in the driveway. It took every ounce of energy I had left, but I gasped out the last word either of us wanted to hear at that moment: "Hurry."

*Thump! Thump!* Just as the front door opened, we slid the cooler into my room and closed the door behind us.

Lloyd knew he couldn't stick around, so he took the secret exit route he used in emergencies like this, out my bedroom window.

"Well," he said, with one foot dangling over my backyard, "you sure are fun to hang out with, Josh."

"Thanks, Lloyd," I replied. "If life sucks after tomorrow, I'll at least be glad we got to be friends first."

Lloyd raised a hand in salute, then leapt out the window into the bushes. "Remember," he called up to me, as he brushed the leaves off his clothes, "the fate of the world rests in your hands. No pressure."

Jerk.

The aliens began to take shape from the grotesque goo in the cooler. I watched them materialize, looking out for any sign of itchy red bumps on their skin. It was hard to tell, since they were still mostly liquid.

"Josh!" My mom was calling me from downstairs. The timing was terrible. Couldn't she wait a minute?

"Josh, are you there?" my dad asked.

I wondered how long I could continue to ignore them. At some point, they'd surely come upstairs. Maybe that would be for the best. If they saw the buttheads, then I could explain everything. I'd tell them how I made the website with Lloyd, how we snuck two aliens out of the ladies' room at Chop Socky in a stolen double stroller, how Doodoofartmama rang up nine hundred dollars in iPhone charges, how they drank my dad's Australian soda and replaced it with a store brand, and how seventy billion more buttheads were just a few light-years away from taking the interstellar off-ramp to Earth.

But they didn't come upstairs. They just waited, calling up to me and sounding a little more disappointed each time I didn't respond. "Josh! Josh?" I think they were worried that I wasn't there like I was supposed to be, but they didn't want to come and check, just in case it was true.

I decided not to wait for the aliens to finish taking shape, and I headed into the hallway. "Hi," I said, glancing downstairs at my parents.

When they saw me, they seemed surprised for a second, and then they smiled. "Hello, son," my dad replied.

I tried to talk, but nothing came out, so I ran downstairs and pulled them both into a tight hug. "I'm really, really sorry," I finally managed to say.

We hugged for a long time, and then my mother backed away. She had something to say, something important it seemed. Was it a message of forgiveness? I looked into her eyes, hopefully, then waited.

"Dinner's in half an hour," she said, at last. Then she turned away and headed toward the kitchen. My dad nodded and followed her, leaving me standing at the base of the staircase, alone.

I desperately wanted a chance to mend my relationship with my parents, but I knew this wasn't the right time. First, I had to check on the buttheads. They'd be back in their bodies by now. I took a deep breath and marched upstairs.

I found the aliens gazing through my telescope at the night sky. I looked up and down their bodies, but there was no sign of chicken pox. They looked perfectly healthy, and more excited than I'd ever seen them.

"We have great news, Josh!" IAmAWeenieBurger announced. "The buttheads are coming!"

They backed away from the telescope to give me a look. Nervously, I peered through the eyepiece at where they had pointed the lens. At first, it looked like an asteroid field, a crowded section of space full of floating rocks and junk. But as my eye adjusted, I realized I was seeing something far more upsetting.

Spaceships.

Thousands of them.

They were different shapes and sizes, some as small as a bus and others as large as the moon. I felt a pit in my stomach, but the buttheads were jumping for joy.

"They're almost here! They're almost here!"

"FRRT! FRRT! FRRT!"

Their excited farts smelled the worst, which only made me feel crummier.

It must've been obvious that I didn't share their joy, because Doodoofartmama stopped jumping and poked IAmAWeenieBurger. "FRRT," he said, gesturing at me with two of his hands.

"Don't be sad," IAmAWeenieBurger said. "You're gonna be the most awesome human on Earth, dude."

"I will?" I said. "What about Quentin? Or Mr. Mudd?"

IAmAWeenieBurger shrugged. "They have flashy titles, but those jobs are just a lot of paperwork. You'll be killing it on the social scene. You were our first Earth host, man, the whole reason our planet-mates came here. You'll be a superstar. Buttheads will be dying to take selfies with you. They'll buy you all the waffles you can eat. They'll make video games about you!"

I hadn't thought about it before, but it did sound kind of cool. When the buttheads got here, I would be famous. They say history is written by the winners. Well, if things went as it seemed like they would, that meant the authors of our next history books would have butt cheeks in their craniums. I would be their Christopher Columbus. Lloyd would be their Benjamin Franklin. We would be the two greatest Earthlings ever, the ones who sold them the deed to this carbon-rich blue boulder wrapped up in breathable air. Forget George Washington or Martin Van Buren. Lloyd Ruggles and Josh McBain would be the names little buttheaded kids would toot out of their jagged green cracks a hundred years from now to win their Smart-Off.

I always got so jealous when people said Quentin was going to change the world. I knew that would never be me. I wasn't special, at least not in a good way. I wasn't a genius or a rock star or even mildly interesting. I was just like most kids, average and ordinary, bound for a run-of-the-mill life where nothing amazing ever happens. But that was about to change. When the aliens arrived, I'd be the most special person ever. I'd be the one on magazine covers. There would be statues of me in new alien cities. I could do anything I wanted.

I could have a sitcom, a talk show, even a cooking show, as long as I learned how to cook first. My autobiography would be a best seller, and schoolkids would do reports on me. If I felt like putting out an album, every superstar in the world would want to work with me. I could duet with Katy Perry or be the new lead singer of Coldplay. I could rap with Jay-Z and Pitbull, and my name would come first in the credits. We'd be listed as "MC-DJ Joshy Fresh Fresh With Jay-Z Featuring Pitbull." I could travel the world—no, the universe even. I could have my own spaceship, and I could ride it to a different water park around the galaxy every week. I'd be the most famous boy who ever lived, because not only would every person on Earth know me, but so would seventy billion buttheads. I'd be unstoppable.

IAmAWeenieBurger and Doodoofartmama must've noticed me smiling, because they went back to celebrating. I took another look in the telescope at all the spaceships just a few planets away from arriving here. They didn't seem so bad now. I started to think of them as swarms of fans, coming to meet me.

I would probably need to start practicing my autograph.

# CHAPTER 18

I fell asleep kind of excited, but after that I had night-mares pretty much the rest of the night. In them, I was surrounded by adoring buttheads with toes that were perfectly picked clean. Then I looked down and noticed that, everywhere we went, we were stomping all over people I knew. Principal Hartley was nothing but a toe-picker, her face squashed under the heel of a butthead police officer. Hiroshi from Chop Socky, too, except he was being stepped on by a butthead ambulance driver. I saw Lloyd's brothers and sisters under some buttheads' feet, all of them fighting for the most comfortable spot. But what really scared me was the sight of my parents. They were lying on a sidewalk, reaching out to every alien toe that passed by. They were miserable, but when they looked up and saw me, their expressions changed to something even worse. It was the same look they had when they saw the nine hundred dollars in iPhone charges and discovered that the soda bottle was filled with supermarket swill.

They were disappointed in me.

I didn't want the aliens to come. I didn't want to be special. I thought about the way my life had always been, and for the first time, it sounded kind of perfect the way it was. I wanted to keep it that way, and to make my parents proud.

The next morning, the sound of my doorknob turning woke me up. That could only mean one thing: a wake-up serenade. For the first time in years, I felt a rush of excitement at the thought. I sat up in bed, ready to sing along, but to my surprise, it wasn't Mom and Dad standing in my doorway.

It was Lloyd.

"Hey, dude! What's up?"

I didn't see how it was possible. Was it not seven o'clock yet? Were my parents still downstairs warming up for their big number? I checked the clock.

7:14.

"What's the matter?" Lloyd asked.

There was only one possibility I could come up with for why they didn't dance on my bed today. "Are my parents dead?"

Lloyd laughed. "No, they're downstairs having breakfast and complaining about having to go to work, just like always."

It wasn't like always, of course. They had left me out of their routine and let me wake up on my own. It was the kind of morning I assumed most kids had. The kind I had always wished for.

It was horrible.

That's when I heard a voice in my head. It was telling me to run downstairs as fast as I could, to throw my arms around my parents and scream, "Mommy! Daddy! Will you sing to me? Please oh please, like you always do?" I wanted to do it, to slide down the bannister with tears in my eyes and beg them to make this just like any other morning. To go back to the way things were, when they trusted me and obsessed over me. When they loved me.

"Go talk to them," Lloyd said.

But I couldn't. Not then. "No, Lloyd," I replied. "First, we have to deal with them." I pointed to my bed, where IAmAWeenieBurger and Doodoofartmama were still glowing underneath the sheets. "I can't believe they slept in."

"Seriously," Lloyd agreed. "Don't they have a planet to take over today?"

When we bent down to check on them, we got a sense of what was making them so tired.

They were sick.

Both of them. They were covered in chicken pox, from butt to toe. Their entire bodies were nothing but a collection of festering red bumps. They had pox on their scaly fronts and pox on their furry backs, on their three hands and all over their toe-noses. And more than anywhere else, they had pox on their butts.

A ton of pox on their butts.

"Dude, your plan worked!" Lloyd said.

The sound of his voice rustled IAmAWeenieBurger from sleep. "Ohhhhhhhhhhh," the alien groaned as he began to stir. He scratched his body with all of his hands at once.

"FRRRRRRRRT," Doodoofartmama groaned.

As they opened their eyes and took in the horrific sight of their own appearance, I tried not to smile or high-five my friend.

"EEEEEEK!" IAmAWeenieBurger shouted. "What happened to us?"

"You're sick," I answered, trying to pass it off like it was no big deal.

"No!" IAmAWeenieBurger said. "Sick is when it's a little hard to breathe and the yucky ooze comes out of your toe-nose. We had that!"

"That's just one kind of sick," Lloyd said. "This is chicken pox."

"Dude, does chicken pox always suck so hard?"

I nodded. "Yeah, but you can only get it once."

"Well, that's a relief, yo!"

"Sure, don't worry," Lloyd said. "The next thing you get will be totally different."

Doodoofartmama rolled all over the floor, trying to scratch every itch on his body.

"The next thing!" IAmAWeenieBurger said. "How many Earth illnesses are there?"

"Oh, I can't count them all," I said. "Strep throat, scurvy, pneumonia."

"Don't forget old-monia," Lloyd interrupted. "And ALS, IBS . . ." He winked at me.

"FBI," I added. "ATM, OMG."

"These are all Earth diseases?" IAmAWeenieBurger asked.

"Oh right," Lloyd said. "Earth Disease. That's another one. And Earth-itis. Earthphobia." He grinned as he continued to make up diseases to scare the aliens.

"Plus that new one, Wiz Khalifa," I added. It was kind of fun. I wasn't just watching Lloyd talk his way out of trouble. I was taking part in it. And I was doing a good job.

IAmAWeenieBurger starting biting his fingernails. "All that stuff is worse than what we have now?"

"Much," Lloyd said. "I was in the hospital with Wiz Khalifa for months."

IAmAWeenieBurger turned to Doodoofartmama, farting frantically. Doodoofartmama farted back at him. They nodded at each other, then turned to me and Lloyd.

"We both agree," IAmAWeenieBurger said. "Your planet sucks."

"FRRT!" Doodoofartmama nodded, then he collapsed into a blob on my floor.

"Doodoofartmama is texting our homies now."

Doodoofartmama sent out another bubble, which seeped through the window and into the sky.

"What's he saying?" I asked.

"He is telling the other buttheads to turn around and go home."

"No, don't leave!" Lloyd said. "You haven't even been through your first hurricane yet. Or earthquake, tsunami, tornado, flash flood, mudslide, wildfire. You've barely seen all the ways Earth can suck."

"I'm sorry, dudes. I know you'll miss us, but we gotta go home so our scientists can cure this. And BTW, how about you not invite any more extraterrestrials here until you've spruced this planet up a bit? No offense."

The bubble returned, seeping through the window back into my room. It was bigger now, its walls pulsing, as if it were a living thing.

"What is that?" I asked.

"That," IAmAWeenieBurger said, "is our ride."

Doodoofartmama resumed his butthead shape and stepped through the bubble. He floated inside it, waving for IAmAWeenieBurger to join him.

"Sorry, man," IAmAWeenieBurger said to me. "You would've had such a kick-butt life if we could've stayed."

"It's OK," I said. "I kind of like my life the way it is."

IAmAWeenieBurger stepped one leg into the bubble, then turned around and looked at me and Lloyd.

"Will you let the Ultimate Supreme President of the Native Residents of Quentonia know that we had to hit the road?"

"Our pleasure," Lloyd replied.

IAmAWeenieBurger stepped fully inside the bubble, and Lloyd and I watched it glide toward the window. But before it seeped outside, IAmAWeenieBurger stuck his head out to say one last thing. "Later, dudes," he said. "You guys are cool. Too bad your planet's so lame."

The bubble floated upward, through the clouds and out of sight. I turned to Lloyd and held my hand out for a high five.

"Darn it," Lloyd said.

"What do you mean?" I asked. "We got rid of them! We saved the planet!"

"Yeah, but I have a history test today, and I didn't study. I thought it'd be canceled due to the alien invasion."

With one problem solved, I was ready to face my parents. "Come on, Lloyd," I said. "I'm not sure this will be so easy."

We found them in the living room, glued to the television. "Wow, that kid is always in the news!" my dad said.[18]

---

18    Read all about it! Our blog post on the news is on page 274.

"He keeps doing such remarkable things," my mom agreed.

On the screen was a live shot of Quentin's house. There were reporters all over his lawn, aiming cameras at him, snapping pictures and holding out microphones. The bottom of the screen read: LOCAL BOY TO DELIVER PROOF OF ALIENS.

Mr. Mudd was there, too, talking to a news crew. "I met the aliens first," he boasted, "back when I was Quentin's age."

To Mr. Mudd's surprise, the reporter seemed kind of annoyed. "But you didn't tell anyone? So why now are you trying to steal his glory?"

Mr. Mudd hung his head in shame. "This is going to be good TV," Lloyd said, elbowing me.

My parents were so caught up in the broadcast, they didn't even notice me and Lloyd behind them. "I never thought aliens were real," my dad said.

My mom shook her head. "He must know what he's doing. I'm sure his parents are proud." Every word she said was like a knife in my back. Not only did my parents not love me anymore, but they had decided to worship my archenemy instead. They were going to feel awfully embarrassed when no aliens showed up.

Among the reporters angling for a good shot of the speech was Kaitlyn Wien-Tomita, who had set up her best camera for the event. "Doesn't that girl go to school here, too?" my dad asked.

"She looks vaguely familiar," my mom said. "Shh! He's starting!"

"Greetings, fellow residents of Earth!" Quentin announced dramatically as he began his press conference. "From the beginning of time, humankind has searched for knowledge of intelligent life in outer space. Today, I not only bring you proof of their existence, I bring you an introduction."

People began to murmur, alarmed. Flashbulbs went off. Quentin waited for the fervor to die down.

"In two minutes time, our extraterrestrial guests will arrive."

Again, the crowd got rowdy, drowning Quentin out with their stunned chatter.

"Aliens are coming now?" my dad said. "No way!"

On screen, Mr. Mudd ran up to the podium, jumping behind the microphone. He was desperate to share in the attention. "I can confirm this," he said. "I met the aliens, too! In fact, I met them first!"

Quentin nudged Mr. Mudd aside. "Naturally, things

will be changing a bit on Earth. There will be seventy billion of them and seven billion of us. But don't worry. I will be looking out for human interests as your new Ultimate Supreme President of the Native Residents of Quentonia."

The reporters began shouting out questions in a frenzy. "Are they peaceful?" "Is this for real?" "What's Quentonia?"

"Excellent questions!" Mr. Mudd said, before Quentin pushed him out of the way again.

"We will have plenty of time to answer your queries as we adjust to the aliens' presence over the next several millennia," Quentin continued. "But since we're only a few moments away from when the sky will fill up with their spaceships, I'll just tell you about the two aliens I've already met. Their appearance will be somewhat surprising to you, as they don't look exactly like us. They're a little shorter, a little furrier, and they have three arms."

Reporters began to murmur and jot down notes. Then Mr. Mudd stepped up to the microphone and added, cheerfully, "Yes! And they have butts in the back of their heads!"

The crowd fell totally silent.

"Is this a joke?" one guy shouted.

Quentin nervously took back the microphone. "I wouldn't joke as your Ultimate Supreme President, I swear. I can assure you, my information is reliable. We've already met two of the aliens."

"What are their names?" someone called out.

Mr. Mudd smiled proudly. "Their names are Doodoofartmama and IAmAWeenieBurger."

The crowd rose up, shouting at Quentin and Mr. Mudd. "You sure are!" one guy yelled. "This is not funny!" said another. "You're trolls!" They were ruthless. When I looked closer, I saw that the "troll" comment was shouted by Principal Hartley. Ouch.

Devastated, Quentin looked to the sky, hoping to see spaceships, but of course, none had shown up.

Lloyd couldn't help laughing. My parents turned around and finally saw us standing there. "That word," my mom said.

"Yeah," my dad agreed, pointing a finger at me. "That's what you said the other day."

"You mean Doodoo—"

"Don't repeat it!" my dad said. "Do you know something about this?"

I didn't know what to say. Thankfully, Lloyd jumped in.

"Yeah, of course. Josh is the one who met the aliens. They were waiting for us in the bathroom of Chop Socky. He brought them home in the trunk of your car, kept them in his room for three days, they rang up nine hundred dollars in charges on his iPhone, drank your soda, ate all the Oreos, then plotted to take over the Earth. Don't worry, though, Josh gave them chicken pox and they called off their plans and flew away in a bubble."

My parents looked at each other for a minute, then they both broke out laughing.

"Hahahaha! You guys are so funny!"

"Wacko, but funny," my dad said, shaking his head.

"So you're not still mad at me?" I asked.

"Oh, Josh, of course not," my mom replied.

"Then why didn't you wake me up today?"

My dad shrugged. "We figured you were getting too old for that."

"Really?"

"Yeah, we're sorry, buddy. It's hard for parents when their baby grows up and he's not so little anymore. I guess we just couldn't accept that."

My mom put her arm around me. "Dad and I talked, and we agreed we need to stop treating you like a child."

It was such a relief. So that's why they'd been less doting the last few days? It wasn't because they'd stopped loving me. They'd actually gained respect for me.

"Does this mean I can charge purchases to my phone without asking?"

"You do, and we'll take your phone away for a month." My dad winked.

On TV, the newscast had returned to the anchor-woman in the studio. I'd never seen a professional newscaster blush before, but she was totally red-faced, bowing her head as if she couldn't bear to look right into the camera. "Apparently, this press conference was nothing but a juvenile hoax. We deeply regret breaking into our regular programming to carry the rantings of a clearly disturbed young man, whose parents must be very, very ashamed."

My mom clicked off the TV just as the newscaster was really laying into Quentin. "Don't get us wrong, Josh. If we're treating you like a grown-up, you need to act like one, too. That means making good choices and being responsible."

"Yeah, no more 'aliens' drinking our soda, OK?" My dad made quote marks with his fingers when he said the word "aliens," just to remind me that he didn't believe me.

"I'm sorry," I said. "I wish I could be perfect, like Quentin."

"Quentin?" my mom said, shocked.

My dad rolled his eyes. "That obnoxious little monster?"

"I thought you liked him," I said.

My dad looked like he might throw up. "Ugh! We can't stand weenie burgers like him!"

"Yeah, nobody can," my mom added.

"So you don't care that I'm not changing the world?"

"Son, you don't have to cure a disease or change the world for us to love you," my dad said.

"All you have to do," my mom added, "is just be Josh."

I heard the voice in my head again, the one telling me to throw my arms around them and scream, "Thanks, Mommy! Thanks, Daddy!" But I didn't do it. I gave them the hug, of course, but that said everything I needed to say.

Lloyd had picked up my laptop and was watching Quentin's press conference again. "You should check this out," he said. "It's insanity!"

"I thought all the news people left."

"This is Kaitlyn's website," he said. "She's the only one still showing the live feed!"

Quentin's press conference had descended into complete chaos. "You will show respect for your Ultimate Supreme President of the Native Residents of Quentonia!" he demanded, as reporters all around him packed up their equipment and started leaving.

"And Your Assistant Undersecretary of Submission and Subservience!" Mr. Mudd added.

"I'm not sure I like you being in that man's science class either," my mom said, shaking her head.

"I think we'd better leave for work," my dad told her.

They walked to the door and put on their coats, then stopped and looked at me.

"There is one childish thing we wanted to do for you," my dad said, "just this one last time."

"Check your lunch box," my mom said with a wink.

And as they did every day, they waved to me all the way down the driveway and as their car pulled down the street and out of sight.

Once they were gone, I peeked in my lunch box to see what they had left for me. It was another lunch note.

This one was a drawing of a goat, with the caption, "You'll always be our little 'kid.'"

I took it out of my lunch box, but this time, I didn't tear it up or hide it. I stuck it on the refrigerator so I would see it every morning. My last ever lunch note. As terrible as all the ones that came before.

And I'd always treasure it.

Meanwhile, Lloyd was calling me frantically from the other room. "Dude, you have to watch this. He's doing a countdown!"

I ran in and saw the live footage from Kaitlyn's website. On my iPhone screen, Quentin was still talking to the few people who remained in his yard. Mr. Mudd was eyeing his watch and glancing periodically at the sky. "The alien invasion begins in 5 . . . 4 . . . 3 . . ." Quentin raised his hands over his head, expecting a wave of spaceships to appear. "2 . . . 1 . . . !"

Silence.

Quentin looked up, but there was no sign of any spaceships. Lloyd and I knew there wouldn't be, of course. All the spaceships were currently headed the other direction.

"Come on out now!" Quentin yelled at the sky. "IAmAWeenieBurger!"

You could see on Kaitlyn's video that the other reporters had all left by then, but she was zooming in for a close-up, as Quentin became even more frantic. "Don't leave the press conference! I have proof! Behold!" He held up the plastic baggie of number four gunk he'd saved.

"Is that silly putty?" a reporter joked, barely glancing at it.

"No, it's the by-product of an alien excretory process! My analysis shows chemicals not present on Earth, proving it comes from extraterrestrial AAAAAAAH!"

Quentin fell behind his podium, and fur flew into the air all around him. "Whoa! What happened?" Lloyd said.

I leaned in for a closer look at the screen. "He's being attacked."

A high-pitched chattering echoed from the TV speakers in surround sound, as Quentin and Mr. Mudd flailed their arms and screamed, "Get off me!" From all around Quentin's yard, hyper gray rodents appeared and jumped into the fray. "Help!" Quentin wailed. As the few remaining spectators stared at him in disbelief, he wriggled around on the ground, shouting, "IAmAWeenieBurger! IAmAWeenieBurger!"

"IAmAWeenieBurger!" Mr. Mudd joined in.

"What's attacking them?" Lloyd asked.

They were small, furry creatures, just like the one we'd seen on the sidewalk the other day. They each had a distinctive burnt sienna glint in their angry eyes. "They're squirrels," I realized. "Insane mutated squirrels."

So this was what happened when they devoured the leftover number four. It turned them into crazy-eyed super-squirrels!

It took three people to pull Quentin and Mr. Mudd free of the attacking horde, and when they stood back up, the baggie that used to have the number four in it was now empty. "No!" Quentin wailed. "It's gone! It's gone!"

Reporters raced back to the scene, rolling cameras and popping flashbulbs, as the squirrels scurried away and Quentin sat down on the ground, in tears. For the first time at Quentin's press conference, something newsworthy had happened. It became the top story all afternoon. "Squirrel Attack at Alien Hoax!"

Once again, Quentin made the front page of the paper. Mr. Mudd was mentioned briefly inside, on page A19.

Lloyd flunked his history test, but I was happy pretty much all day about the way things played out with the buttheads. We got to hang out with aliens, and we didn't doom our planet in the process. Go us. At the end of the day, we tracked down Kaitlyn at her locker to compliment her on her excellent camerawork.

"Yeah, we finally got revenge on Quentin," she said, high-fiving us.

"You mean, you were trying to get revenge on him, too?" Lloyd asked.

"Duh," she said. "Don't you remember at my eighth birthday party when he barfed ice cream cake all over my Purse Puppies? Why did you think I was always following him around with my camera? To record your aliens?"

"You mean . . . you knew about the aliens?"

"Of course," Kaitlyn said. "I read your blog. And I got plenty of footage of the buttheads while I was recording Quentin."

"So you were the fourth like!" I said. "But if you had footage of them, why didn't you post it? That would've gotten you so many hits."

"Yeah, and possibly had us all picking out toe jam for the rest of time." Kaitlyn gave us a look. "I heard that, too." She slung her backpack over her shoulder and headed for the bike rack. "Later, guys."

As we watched her go, I realized there were plenty of cool people here on Earth, and maybe next time Lloyd and I had an urge to meet some aliens, we should try to get to know some of the people here instead.

# EPILOGUE[19]

After his disastrous press conference, Quentin made the cover of *Newsweek* again. "Too Successful Too Young?" read the headline. It was all about kids who'd done something amazing when they were little and been built up like they were bound to rule the world someday. Almost all of them spent the rest of their lives trying to recapture that glory and failing repeatedly. After it came out, a lot of newspapers vowed to stop doing those "Kids Who Are Changing the World" stories and just let kids be kids. Quentin, on the other hand, vowed to do something even bigger and better

---

19   An epilogue is the part at the end of the book that no one ever reads, but you should read this one, because it wraps up the story pretty well. Also, read our blog on books, on page 276, especially if you wish this book wasn't over just yet.

next time, and to destroy me and Lloyd in the process. So we have that to look forward to.

After the whole TV meltdown, Mr. Mudd stopped teaching science and wrote a book about the aliens. Not many people believed it, but the few people who did became totally obsessed with him and treated him like a hero. He began devoting all his time to attending alien conventions, where he often appeared in a butthead costume and taught classes on how to speak in farts.

The real surprise was what happened to Kaitlyn. Her reports about Quentin and his meltdown got tens of millions of hits. She got so popular online that the local TV station hired her to do a kids' report for the five o'clock news. She never made anyone's list of future superstars, but she found something she liked to do and was good at, and she worked hard at it. Lloyd and I watched her every time she was on, between Johnny Touchdown's Fumble Follies and Tommy Tornado's Wacky Weather.

I've always known that only a few people get to be super geniuses, but for the first time I realized that it's OK to be one of the other people. I resigned from the Smart-Off team, because I hadn't earned it, and

Quentin got to be the Super Brain again. It was only fair, and it kept him busy so he didn't bug me and Lloyd too much. The two of us joined the bowling league. We came in dead last, and we had a blast.

So I was an unpopular sixth grader? At least it was better than being a popular dung beetle. Even if you're the coolest dung beetle in the world, you're still eating poop all day. When I thought of it that way, I was satisfied with my life. Sure, the people who are freakishly good at one thing or another get all the attention. But with that comes all the pressure. Nobody was expecting me to cure cancer or become president or host a TV cooking show. All I had to do was just keep on living, and as long as I did, who knows what might happen.

Lloyd and I vowed not to invite any more aliens to Earth. We just went back to playing bike hockey in the parking lot of the Mexican fast food place that had to close after all the bacteria outbreaks. That was how we spent our time, playing games and hanging out, and it was the absolute best.

Anyway, as far as changing the world, we'd been there and done that, even if no one but Quentin, Mr. Mudd, and Kaitlyn would ever know.

# APPENDIX

THE PEACEFUL EXTRATERRESTRIAL'S
GUIDE TO EARTH
by Lloyd and Josh,
Earthlings

http://peacefulextraterrestrialsguidetoearth.freeblogz.biz/holidays/

# Holidays

There are lots of days on our planet where people throw parties, appliance stores have big sales, and most importantly, we get the day off from school. One of them is the day this guy Abraham Lincoln was born, because he did lots of great things and then died watching a play, which is just about the worst way to go. When you come to Earth, don't see any plays. Trust us. They're horrible.

The best holiday of all is probably Christmas, which is when humans bring a tree indoors, then they run really old cartoons on TV and parents finally buy kids all the things they've been saying "no" to all year. Christmas usually falls about three weeks after they release the new Xbox.

Then there's another day everyone celebrates, which isn't technically a holiday. It's called a birthday, and it happens once every time the Earth circles around the sun, on the day you were born. Birthdays are great unless they fall around Christmas, because then a person's two biggest present-getting days end up mushed into one, and they have to wait a whole year to get anything else off their wish list.

There was once a guy named Jesus who was supposedly born on Christmas Day. Man, he got a raw deal.

Posted by Lloyd and Josh, September 14 at 7:38 pm
Likes: 4
Comments: 0

## Inventions

Humans are really proud of the things we've invented, like fire and light bulbs, and deep frying foods that aren't normally deep fried. The truth is, though, that next to iPhones, all of those other inventions are complete garbage. That's because iPhones are pretty much every other worthwhile invention rolled into one. They're a camera, a calculator, and best of all, a way to stream skateboarding fail videos during lame school assemblies.

Grown-ups also use iPhones to make these things called "phone calls," which was how people kept in touch before Thomas Edison invented texting. Phone calls are conversations where every other sentence is, "What? You're cutting out! Hello? Hello?" Also, there are no emojis on phone calls, so it's impossible to tell what anyone's really thinking.

iPhones are so much a part of life that life without an iPhone is absolute torture. You might see people laughing at a picture and saying, "I am so Instagramming that!" If you have an iPhone, you can look it up right away, but if not, you never find out what was so funny. Or if you overhear someone say, "Did you hear about Katy Perry?" an iPhone helps you find out right away whether she has a new single or she's dead.

Posted by Lloyd and Josh, September 17 at 4:51 pm
Likes: 4
Comments: 0

## Bathrooms

When Earthlings have to poop or pee, we go to a place called a bathroom. "Bathroom" is kind of a dumb word for it, because we don't usually take a bath there, but I guess no one wanted to call it a pooproom. They were probably afraid kids would laugh every time someone asked the teacher for a pooproom pass. Or maybe some fancy adult was worried about getting all dressed up for the opera or something and then having to say, "Pardon me, but might you kindly direct me to the pooproom?"

After we finish going to the bathroom, we flush the toilet, and the poop and pee are taken to the ocean, where they become the fishes' problem. They always say it's bad to drink seawater, and it's pretty clear why: because seawater is made up of 90% fish pee. Think about it. How could it not be? If fish were smart, they'd invent plumbing that dumped all their waste products on land. But their brains are about the size of rabbit turds, so instead we get to dump all our pee on them, and it swirls around with their pee in the biggest toilet in the universe. This is also why people shouldn't eat sea salt.

Lloyd says: If my dad was naming bathrooms, they might be called "libraries," since he always takes a newspaper in there to read while he does his business. I think seeing what the president is doing with his tax dollars helps his poop come out faster or something.

Posted by Lloyd and Josh, September 19 at 1:04 pm
Likes: 4
Comments: 0

# Games

Humans love to play games. At first, games were stupid, like cavemen seeing who could stare at a rock the longest. (Spoiler alert: Grok won.) Later, games were ways for moms to keep their kids busy so they could drink wine and talk to their friends on the phone. Eventually, people made moms feel bad about this, so moms came up with this thing called Family Game Night, where they forced their husband and kids to bond while eating microwave popcorn and playing games from the 1950s. There's one called "Life," where you pretend to be a person who's living a life, which is exactly what you'd be doing if you weren't wasting your time playing the stupid game.

Most families eventually stop doing family game night. Usually, this comes around the time the dad realizes the kids are old enough that he doesn't have to let them win anymore. Right after this, the kids start to realize their dad is a hyper-competitive jerk. No one needs to hear their father shout "Boo-yah!" every time he passes "Go" in Monopoly. That's when the mom realizes she'd rather be on the phone drinking wine again, and family game night comes to an end.

Josh says: My dad let me win at checkers until I was ten. It would've ended sooner, but I didn't realize he was letting me win. I thought my dad was just really, really bad at checkers, and I felt sorry for him. So around when I was eight, I started trying to let my dad win. The games would take hours. Finally, one night, I got so frustrated that I shouted out, "I've been trying to let you win!" And my dad replied, "*I've* been trying to let *you* win!" Then we both agreed checkers was a dumb game, and we never played it again.

Posted by Lloyd and Josh, September 19 at 3:03 pm
Likes: 4
Comments: 0

## Old Ladies

Old ladies are pretty much the greatest people on Earth. Sure, they smell weird and they pinch kids' cheeks, but they also let kids do things their parents won't, like eat hot fudge sundaes for dinner and play M-rated video games. (The key is convincing them that "M" stands for "Math.")

There are a few things no one should ever do with an old lady, though. One is to get in a car when an old lady is driving. They are very slow, and it's impossible to hear the radio over the sound of the other drivers honking at them. Also, never eat their chocolate chip cookies, because they're guaranteed to contain nuts, raisins, celery, or something else that totally ruins them. Old ladies don't understand the kinds of foods kids like.

More than anything else, though, the number one thing not to do with an old lady is to get into a conversation with one. Old ladies get tired doing just about everything else in the world, but somehow, talking to kids never wears them out. First, they will ask us about school. Then, they will ask why we never wear the sweater they bought us for Christmas. Then they will talk about all the medical problems they have. This is why the average length of an old lady conversation is approximately forever.

Josh says: I have two grandmas. We call them Grandma Cuckoo and Grandma Nutjob. It's not what it sounds like, though. Grandma Cuckoo earned her nickname because she has a loud cuckoo clock in her apartment. Grandma Nutjob is called that because she used to work at the Planters Peanut factory. Also, they're both totally wacko.

Posted by Lloyd and Josh, September 19 at 1:38 pm
Likes: 4
Comments: 0

# Being Sick

Being sick is usually a good thing.

Doing a cool trick on a skateboard is sick. Playing a prank on a substitute teacher is sick. Wearing a T-shirt with Hello Kitty as a skull that has a snake coming out of its eye sockets is super sick. When someone says someone is sick, it's a compliment—with one exception, which is when a doctor says it.

When a doctor tells an Earthling we're sick, it means we're headed for Puke City. Getting that kind of sick is about the least sick thing possible.

We're not sure why doctors use the word "sick" to mean something bad, when everyone else agrees "sick" is good. It must suck, because doctors can't use the word "sick" in a cool way like the rest of us. Otherwise, they might end up saying something like, "Hey, man, that new liver we gave you is totally sick!" and their patient would think he was going to die.

For humans, there's one good thing about being sick in a doctor-type way, which is that we get to stay home from school. It's like an unexpected holiday, where we can stay in our pajamas and play on the iPad all day. There are only two things that can ruin a good sick day. One is if we're too sick to enjoy it. If a person spends long enough bent over a toilet barfing their guts out, pretty soon, they'll wish they were back at school dividing fractions.

The other thing that can ruin a sick day is if, when we get back, our teacher makes us catch up on all the work we missed while we were gone. It's not fair. When teachers are out sick, no one makes them go back and write all the hall passes they would've given out if they'd been in school.

Posted by Lloyd and Josh, September 19 at 11:01 pm
Likes: 4
Comments: 0

# Sleep

Humans sleep about one third of their lives, which you might think is kind of a waste, until we tell you that nothing good is on TV at night and no one else is awake anyway, except really creepy animals, like bats and owls and Josh's neighbor who has tinfoil on his windows and who Josh's dad says he's "keeping an eye on."

When humans sleep, almost everything in our bodies keeps working. Our lungs keep breathing, our stomach keeps digesting, and our heart keeps pumping blood. Unfortunately, our brains pretty much conk out the whole time, so we can't use them for anything productive. It'd be cool if people could spend their sleep hours doing all the stuff they don't want to waste time on during the day, like sit-ups and reading classics of American literature for English and Language Arts. When kids wake up, sometimes their parents ask them how they slept, which is pretty much the dumbest question in the world. We wish when our parents asked that question, we could answer something like, "It was great. I ran a 5K and finally got to the end of *Anne of Green Gables.*"

Mostly, people sleep at home in their beds, but another great place to do it is in Mrs. Michaelson's social studies

**257**

class. She's so boring, sometimes, she puts herself to sleep. We've still never heard how World War I ended.

Posted by Lloyd and Josh, September 19 at 2:16 pm
Likes: 4
Comments: 0

## Curses

We have special words on Earth that we can only use
on certain cable channels and when our parents are not
around. Some people call them curses or swears or dirty
words. If you come here, we'll teach you all the ones we
know, and if you have any on your planet, we'd love to hear
them, because we could use them in school and the teachers would never know what we were saying. "A pop quiz?
Gleebleglork!" That'd be sweet.

Usually people save curses for when they're really mad or
excited, but rock stars are required to curse at least once
every five words they say. Instead of "We're about to go on
tour," a rock star might say, "We're about to go on cursing
tour." Or "We're hitting the cursing road." Or "Cursey curse
curse a city near you." That's why rock stars are our mod-
ern-day poets.

Nobody wants little kids to find out what the curses are,
especially not the really good ones. If there's a lot of cursing
in a movie, it gets rated PG-13, which means most parents
won't let their kids see it until they're nine or ten. If a movie
has a lot of cursing and they show boobs, too, then it's rated
R, which means no one under seventeen is allowed to see
it until it comes on Netflix and their parents go out for the
night.

Josh says: In third grade, my mom helped me with a school report about beavers, and she kept saying, "the water blockage structure" because she couldn't bring herself to use the word "dam." On the day before the report was due, I said, "I'm so water blockage structure tired of writing about beavers." I got grounded for that, which I don't think was fair.

Posted by Lloyd and Josh, September 19 at 8:58 pm
Likes: 4
Comments: 0

# Fights

People on Earth fight. A lot.

Sometimes, people fight over actual things like parking spaces or the last slice of pizza. Other times, they fight over ideas, like which diet cola has the most refreshing low-calorie taste or whether or not a certain quarterback is a bum. Pretty much every human encounter can turn into a fight without warning.

Sometimes, fights get really big, and we call them wars. Instead of our fists, we fight with guns and bombs. You might think since the weapons are bigger that wars are about more important things than regular fights. But usually, wars are fought over dumb things like where the border between WhoCares-istan and The Republic of Loserface lies, or which religion is more peaceful.

Josh says: There are some people who don't like fighting of any kind. They're called moms. My mom won't even let me fight in video games. She gets really upset when she sees me trying to get my Yoshi to slap Pikachu around in New Pork City, even though all she's really looking at are a bunch of zeroes and ones on a computer and not even a microchip is getting the tiniest boo-boo.

Posted by Lloyd and Josh, September 20 at 9:08 am
Likes: 4
Comments: 0

# School

Birds have the right idea about school. When they get old enough, their mom pushes them out of the nest, and the bird has about three seconds to either figure out how to fly or become a bird waffle in somebody's backyard. That's all there is to bird school.

Humans only know a tiny bit more than birds, but they make school go on forever by studying dumb things like English, which is the language we already speak, and history, which is a bunch of stuff that already happened. History is probably the worst subject, because it's about a bunch of dead people, and there's more to know about it every year. Someday, kids will spend so long learning history, they won't have any time to make a future.

You'll sometimes hear old people on Earth complain, "Youth is wasted on the young." But the truth is, most of youth is wasted in school, and most old people waste too much time complaining.

Humans really don't know enough to fill up twelve years of education, so we made up a bunch of subjects just to keep kids busy, like trigonometry, where we spend two whole marking periods learning about triangles, and geography, where we're forced to memorize the capitals of countries we'll never go to and which may not even exist. Chad? Really? That was the best name some country could come up with for itself? We're really supposed to believe that a bunch of people in Africa go around saying, "Hi. I live in Chad"? More likely, there's some guy named Chad who works at the map company who managed to sneak that by his boss. Someday, geography teachers around the world are going to figure out what happened, and Chad will totally get fired for it.

Posted by Lloyd and Josh, September 19 at 9:41pm
Likes: 4
Comments: 0

## Photos

Earthlings take a lot of photos, probably because everything from phones to doorbells to waffle irons have cameras in them these days. A long time ago, when the world was in black and white, cameras cost a ton of money, and some people might only get one picture of themselves taken in their lifetime. They'd get all dressed up and try to look really serious and dignified for it, and then, they wouldn't even know until they got it developed whether they were blinking or if they had a booger.

Abraham Lincoln took as many pictures in his whole life as the average person takes of their lunch on any given day. Lincoln's pictures would hang up in the National Gallery, and maybe a thousand tourists would get to see them. Today, a tuna fish sandwich can get a million likes on Instagram within five minutes.

The only thing people like photographing more than their food is themselves. We call them "selfies," and we take them all the time, just so we can share pictures of ourselves with our friends, who already know what we look like anyway. It's hard to imagine what the world would've been like if there were selfies when Abraham Lincoln was alive. The Smithsonian would have framed pictures of his social media posts where he's signing the Emancipation Proclamation with one hand and giving the peace sign with the other. There'd be a caption that said, "Freed the slaves. What did YOU do today? #MakingHistory."

Josh says: My mom has so many pictures of me on her phone from when I was little that I could literally spend the rest of my life looking at them if I wanted to. If you pulled any of these pictures up and asked me to tell you what was happening when it was taken, I would probably say, "I was begging my mom to stop taking pictures of me."

Posted by Lloyd and Josh, September 19 at 10:37 pm
Likes: 4
Comments: 0

## Punishments

When Earthlings get in trouble, they get punished. If they
do something really bad, they get arrested and go to jail. Jail
is a place full of cinder block walls, terrible food, and horrible people, and no one is allowed to leave. So it's basically
school, only better, because they don't force the people in
jail to learn anything.

If a kid does something bad, they'd better hope it's bad
enough to get them sent to jail. Otherwise, they get punished by their parents, who can do really horrible things, like
send kids to bed without dessert or take away their iPhone.

Parents like to let kids know how much worse they got punished when they were young. They'll remind them that they
didn't even have Xboxes or iPhones for their parents to take
away from them. It's actually a really good point: when they
were kids, just being alive was punishment enough.

Lloyd says: Punishment in my house is a little different. Since
all my brothers and sisters and me share bedrooms, it's not
really a punishment to get sent there, because there's always
someone else around. So instead, when one of us gets in
trouble, we have to go to the kitchen and listen to our mom

tell stories about her job while she cooks dinner. I try never to get in trouble, because I hate listening to my mom drone on about her office, although I agree with her that Marcy from human resources is on a bit of a power trip.

Posted by Lloyd and Josh, September 20 at 9:48 am
Likes: 4
Comments: 0

**Parents**

One of the biggest challenges for those of us living on Earth is putting up with our parents. They speak their own language, which only they understand. They say things that make absolutely no sense, like, "Because I said so!" and "I paid for that!" and "When I was your age, I thought I knew everything, too!" Sometimes they laugh and high-five each other when they say these things. Parents love parent jokes. No one else does.

Parents come in lots of different combinations. Most people have one mom and one dad, but Carl Polito-Montoya has two dads, and they're pretty much the coolest family ever because they own every gaming system and they never have to put the toilet seat down. It's also possible to have two moms, or one mom and no dad, or one dad and no mom. Some people have birth parents and adoptive parents. Some have stepparents or foster parents, or they're raised by their grandparents or by wolf parents in the wilderness. It really doesn't matter, because they're all terrible.

Josh says: Parents like to save stuff from when you were little, like this Mother's Day card I made my mom in kindergarten. She had it until last year, when she finally realized that I'd spelled out her name entirely in boogers. On the plus side, I found out how durable boogers are as a crafting material.

Posted by Lloyd and Josh, September 25 at 4:11 pm
Likes: 4
Comments: 0

## Aliens

This is not easy to say, but we have to confess that most humans are under the assumption that you aliens are a bunch of donkey-butt jerks.

Just look at the movies Earthlings have made. Aliens are always zapping us with laser guns, or eating us, or popping out of our stomachs in a geyser of guts. In our minds, the only reason an extraterrestrial species would evolve, master quantum physics, devote endless resources to building a spaceship, and then endure the long, unforgiving journey through the nothingness of space is so that they can make Will Smith's life miserable. Yes, we're ashamed to admit it, but humans are alienist.

Alien-phobic.

We can guarantee this, though: there are at least two humans who are hoping that aliens will prove everyone wrong and be peaceful, and that's us.

Well, maybe there are three, because we'd bet after all he's been through in his movies, Will Smith would probably get on board with that, too.

Another thing you should know about Earthlings is that we're terrible at naming things. For example, there's a type of fish we call catfish, named for two animals that are mortal enemies: cats and fish. Then there's a species of sharks we named nurse sharks: because if there's one thing the fiercest animal in the ocean wants, it's to be associated with the lady at school who's only allowed to give out Band-Aids or let us lie down for ten minutes if we fake a tummy ache. If you actually come to Earth, there's a good chance we'll start calling you "Galaxius creaturus boringus" or "Species 42E69F," or worse, some big-headed scientist will name you after his dopey kid. "They came here from across the cosmos," he'll say, when he introduces you. "Presenting . . . the Sweet Little Ashleys!"

Posted by Lloyd and Josh, September 22 at 5:01 pm
Likes: 4
Comments: 0

# Friends

The only way we Earthlings can put up with all the donkey-butt jerks of the world is if we have really cool friends. We can complain to our friends about our parents, and they'll make us feel better by telling us about the things their parents do that are even worse.

Most friends are people we've actually met in real life, but there are other kinds of friends, too, like the ones we met online playing *Gears of War* once like six months ago who still send us party requests at weird hours almost every day. Friends have names like Mike or Malik or BoomGoezDaDynamite4827!&#.

We never have to be embarrassed around our friends, and we can tell them all our secrets, like our email password in case we get hit by a bus and we need them to go in and delete all our old messages before our parents find them.

Lloyd says: By the way, Josh, if I ever get hit by a bus . . .

Josh says: I'm on it, buddy.

Posted by Lloyd and Josh, September 25 at 8:02 pm
Likes: 4
Comments: 0

http://peacefulextraterrestrialsguidetoearth.freeblogz.biz/vaccines/
# Vaccines

When humans get sick, we take medicine, which eventually helps us feel better. Sometimes, we fight against a disease before we even get it, by taking a vaccine. A vaccine actually gives a person a small amount of a virus so our bodies will recognize it and learn how to fight against it, in case it ever tries to attack us again. It sounds like a pretty good deal, but the way doctors give us a vaccine is by sticking a giant needle in our arm.

When you really think about it, it makes no sense. There are so many perfectly fine openings in a human body already. Why do doctors always need to make new ones with sharp objects just to cram medicine in there? If doctors are smart enough to invent vaccines, they should be able to come up with a way to give people one by rubbing it on their toes or making an ice cream out of it, rather than by violently jabbing their patients with metal. The fact that they insist on using needles is probably just a sign that the medical profession attracts people who happen to like needles. If you ask doctors what their hobbies are outside of work, most of them will probably say knitting and inflating basketballs.

That's what's really sick, and not in the good way.

Posted by Lloyd and Josh, September 26 at 11:11 am
Likes: 4
Comments: 0

# News

People on Earth love to know what's going on in other parts of Earth. So we watch the news. That's where people on television with perfect skin and hair, called "reporters," share stories and videos from other places so that we can see what's going on there without actually having to go there ourselves.

There's so much news that some TV channels show nothing but news twenty-four hours a day. These are the channels our grandparents watch when they come to visit. Anywhere there's a TV tuned to a news channel, you can bet that only a few feet away, there's a kid who'd rather be playing Xbox. When the news channels run out of news to report, they put on shows where loud people yell at each other about politics. You would think that by now, all these yelling people would've solved a few of the world's problems, but instead, this planet is more messed up than ever.

Josh says: There's only one news channel my Grandma Nutjob will watch. It's the one that talks about the president the way teenage girls talk about boy bands. They always say how great he is and how anyone who doesn't like him is just a hater and a liar and probably likes really lame forms of government, like communism, those losers! Whenever anyone says anything bad about the president, Grandma

Nutjob throws hard candies at the TV. Grandma Cuckoo only watches one news channel, too, but she likes the one that talks about the president the way teenage *boys* talk about boy bands. They only say how much he sucks and how people who like him are dum-dums and how they can't even stand to listen to him for five seconds without wanting to throw up. She, too, throws hard candies at the TV when the president's face comes on.

Whenever Grandma Nutjob and Grandma Cuckoo talk to each other, they raise their voices and accuse each other of being "brainwashed" a lot. My family tries never to invite them both over at the same time, and on the rare occasions that we do, my mom has me hide all the hard candies.

Posted by Lloyd and Josh, September 26 at 12:12 pm
Likes: 4
Comments: 0

## Books

When an Earthling wants to learn about something, a good way to do it is by reading a book. Some books are non-fiction, which means they include real facts, like how to fix a car engine, or fun things to do in Uruguay. Then there's fiction, which are books full of stuff that someone just made up. That might sound really dumb, to spend your time getting involved with characters who aren't real and stuff that didn't actually happen, but it's just about the best thing you can do.

In a book, anything can happen. Tree houses can become time machines. Two boys can brainwash their principal into thinking he's a superhero who fights crime in his under-pants. Kids with magic powers can go to a special school in England where people have owls for pets and everything has funny names. Pretty much any random thing some weirdo can think up. And it's awesome. When you read a book, you get to hang out with cool people and learn about the crazy adventures they have. Books can be scary or sad or funny and sometimes romantic, although we don't recommend those books unless you want to barf all over the pages at the really mushy parts.

That's one more cool thing about books. Even at the worst times, a good book can make things a little bit better. If there's one thing that sucks about books, it's when you're reading one you really like, and it ends.

Posted by Lloyd and Josh, March 18 at 4:44 pm
Likes: 4
Comments: 0

# ABOUT THE AUTHOR

**Jerry Mahoney** is the author of the series My Rotten Stepbrother Ruined Fairy Tales. He is located in the city of Los Angeles on the planet Earth, along with a husband and two children who are most likely human. His butt is just where you'd expect it to be, thank you very much. Find out more at jerrymahoneybooks.com.